SUSAN GOLDMAN RUBIN

Emily Good
as Gold

BROWNDEER PRESS

HARCOURT BRACE & COMPANY

San Diego   New York   London

Requests for permission to make copies of any
part of the work should be mailed to:
Permissions Department,
Harcourt Brace & Company, 8th Floor,
Orlando, Florida 32887.

Library of Congress Cataloging-in-Publication
Data available upon request.

ISBN 0-15-276632-4
ISBN 0-15-276633-2 pbk.

Printed in Hong Kong

Designed by Lori J. McThomas

First edition

ABCDE

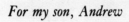

For my son, Andrew

I want to thank the following people for helping me with this book: Sonia Levitin, Eve Bunting, Mary Daegling, Kay Haugaard, Tony Johnston, Lael Littke, Gloria Miklowitz, Martha Tolles, Elizabeth Van Steenwyk, and, especially, the late Helen Hinckley Jones. I'd also like to thank Stanley J. Leiken, M.D., Clinton Y. Montgomery, M.D., Noel Nyman, and the students, parents, and staff of the Sophia T. Salvin School in Los Angeles.

My thanks to Andrea Brown and Linda Zuckerman for believing in this book. And most of all, I thank my husband, Michael, for involving me in this project in the first place.

Emily Good
as Gold

Best wishes,

Susan Goldman Rubin

1

EMILY KNEW EXACTLY WHY HER BROTHER AND Phyllis didn't have a big wedding. It was because of her. She would have spoiled it. The people who didn't know her would have stared at her the way they always did and asked the same dumb questions. *Can she read and write? How old is she? Thirteen? But she doesn't look as though anything's wrong with her. She's pretty.*

Emily remembered perfectly the day she first heard the news about the wedding. She was at Camp Pleasant Lake, the camp she went to every summer. All the kids there were like her. They were in the dining hall eating lunch when an announcement came over the loudspeaker.

"Long-distance call for Emily Gold."

Her best friend Molly squealed, "That's you!"

Emily put down her fork. Excitement momentarily took away her appetite. She had never had a telephone call at camp before. Usually her parents printed letters she could read by herself, and sometimes they sent packages of comic books, stickers, and yo-yos.

"You'd better hurry," her counselor said.

Emily ran past the other tables to the knotty pine office where Mitzi, the camp secretary, handed her the receiver. "It's your mother."

"Mommy?"

"How are you, darling?"

"Fine."

"What did you do today?"

"Played basketball and went to arts and crafts."

"That sounds like fun," her mother said. "Hold on. Daddy wants to say hello."

"Hi, sugar. How's my baby girl?"

"Daddy, we did potato prints today. I made a picture of you."

"Thanks, sweetheart. I'll hang it up in my shop when you come home. Are you getting enough to eat?"

"Yes," Emily laughed.

Her father was the one who brought home

treats—pink cake boxes full of chocolate cake and cookies with sprinkles, grocery bags full of corned beef and pickles. He loved to see his family eat. Even when they were full he'd say, "Go on. Have some more—it won't hurt you."

Her mother said it was lucky Emily never got fat like Paula and some of the other girls at her camp and school.

"We're having tuna fish salad for lunch," Emily told her father.

"Good. Here's Mommy."

She got back on the phone and said, "Emily, we have some wonderful news. Tom's getting married."

"Married."

"To a very nice girl named Phyllis. I know you're going to like her."

For a minute Emily was too surprised to say anything. Her brother, Tom, was the person she adored most in the world. He was so smart. Her parents were always talking about the way he had graduated third in his class at law school. But he still found time to joke with her and tell her stories and play games. He was always teaching her things—how to ride a two-wheeler, play Ping-Pong and poker. He had even promised to teach her how to Electric Slide, a new dance, when she came home from camp.

Now her mother rattled on. "Tom and Phyllis love each other very much. They're getting married tomorrow."

"Will I be a flower girl?" Emily's favorite picture in her head was herself at Tom's wedding. She would wear a long pink dress that touched the floor. The bride would wear a white gown and veil. Tom would be in a tuxedo. There would be a band playing music, flowers everywhere, and a tall wedding cake with little bride and groom dolls on top.

"No, dear." Her mother hesitated. "It's going to be a very small wedding."

Emily felt her lower lip quiver. She tried not to cry. She stared at the calendar on Mitzi's desk but all she could think of was how she would have looked in her long pink dress.

"Emily, honey," her mother said slowly, "I'm sorry. You're not going to be at the wedding."

Emily was stunned. Phyllis must have heard about her from Tom and her parents and had decided to get married before Emily came home from camp. That way Emily wouldn't be around to embarrass her. Mommy must have told her Emily was *special*. Lately she hated that word. It meant her head didn't work right. It set her apart from everyone else in her family.

When Tom's girlfriends came over they pretended to be nice but Emily knew how they really felt about her. One time a girl with straight yellow hair and lots of makeup came to dinner and gave her a piece of bubble gum. She smiled a stupid smile as though Emily were two years old. Then she asked Tom a lot of dumb questions even though Emily was sitting right there. *Can she understand us? Does she go to a special school? Why does she look so blank?*

Later, when Emily was helping her mother clear the table, she asked her what blank was.

"Empty, like a piece of paper with nothing on it. Why do you ask?"

Emily didn't tell her. Blank. The word rang in her head every time she looked at herself in the mirror or caught her reflection in a store window.

"Emily," her mother said now, "are you still there?"

"I want to come to the wedding."

"There's no time for me to come and get you."

"I can take the train."

"Not by yourself, dear. It's a six-hour trip."

"Let me talk to Tom!" Emily shouted.

"He and Phyllis are out getting their license."

"What's that?"

Her mother sighed. "It's too hard to explain on the phone. We'll talk more about it when you come home. Have a good time at camp, darling. Maybe you'll make Mommy something nice."

In the cabin Emily pushed aside her Snoopy autograph hound and favorite doll, Gumdrop, and threw herself on her cot. When Molly came in she sat down on her cot beside Emily's.

"Why are you crying?" she asked.

"My brother's getting married."

"Are you going to be the flower girl?"

"No," Emily sobbed. She felt the hurt all over again. "I'm not even going to be there."

Molly chewed thoughtfully on the end of one of her long red braids. "What's the girl look like?"

"Her name is Phyllis."

Molly reached into the orange crate that was her cubbyhole and pulled out a *Seventeen* magazine. One of the things Emily liked about Molly was that she knew what to wear and had the best clothes in their cabin. Cute matching outfits. Halters, shorts, jeans, off-the-shoulder peasant blouses. The kind of clothes you'd see in a magazine. Molly said they were her sister's hand-me-downs and not so great, but Emily secretly wished she had a sister who would give *her* hand-me-downs.

Once Molly let her borrow a khaki shirt with tabs on the shoulders and sleeves that rolled up and buttoned. Wearing that shirt, Emily felt like a different person—a normal, regular, real, thirteen-year-old teenage girl. At bedtime she reluctantly took it off and gave it back to Molly. It felt as though she were giving up the person she wanted to be.

Now Molly flipped through the pages and stopped at a picture of a girl in a white bikini. "I bet she looks like this."

Emily sat up, wiping her eyes, and studied the page.

"You know," Molly said slyly, "Phyllis is going to be taking her top off."

"No, she won't," Emily said. "Tom wouldn't want her to do that."

"Oh, Emily, that's why people get married. And your brother's going to take his pants off."

Emily's face grew hot. "He will not!"

"He will too, and pretty soon they'll have a baby."

"How do you know?" Emily screamed. "He's *my* brother!"

Molly's eyes narrowed. "Because my sister told me. Emily, you're going to have to take your top off in front of a boy if you ever want to have a baby."

Emily gasped. "That's not true!"

"It is so," Molly said, tossing her braids with authority. "How do you think you get babies, huh?"

She had no idea. All she knew was that she wanted a baby of her own when she grew up. A baby to hug and kiss and cuddle. A baby to love her back and call her Mommy. When she got her first period last year her mother explained again that her body was getting ready to have babies. She was thrilled. Now it was only a matter of time.

"I get my period," she reminded Molly.

"Oh, Emily, you're so dumb. What's that got to do with it? It's the way I told you. And there's more." She whispered something so awful Emily got mad and hit her. She ran out of the cabin and the screen door banged shut behind her.

What if Molly was right? Emily thought. She seemed so sure. What if Tom and Phyllis did have a baby? Then everyone would know what disgusting things they had done.

Grinding her teeth Emily thought, It's Phyllis's fault. Why did she have to come along and marry Tom anyway? I hate Phyllis.

2

MANY DAYS LATER EMILY'S GROUP WAS HAVING relay races when Mitzi came along. Emily took her turn and ran to the chair and sat hard on the blue balloon. It popped.

"Yay!" Molly shouted. She jumped up and down waiting for Emily to run back and tag her.

"Emily," called Gloria, her counselor, "you have visitors. Go up to the office with Mitzi."

Who could the visitors be? Only her mother and father ever came to see her at camp.

On the way to the office Mitzi said, "Boy, are you popular. Imagine your brother and sister-in-law stopping to see you on their honeymoon."

Emily's throat went dry. Her heart thumped. She hadn't expected to see Tom and

Phyllis today. What would Phyllis be like? Probably mean, like Tom's other girlfriends. She'd talk to Emily in a dumb way or not talk to her at all. Or show off in a cute dress and cross her legs a lot.

If only she weren't wearing her old seersucker shorts and camp T-shirt from last summer! Those clothes made her look like a baby. Maybe she could run back to the cabin and change. Borrow Molly's khaki shirt. But it was too late. She and Mitzi were already at the road.

There, standing near his car, were Tom and a girl almost his height. Emily ran straight into her brother's arms and hugged him tight.

He kissed the top of her head and then he said, "Emily, this is Phyllis."

There had to be a mistake. Phyllis didn't look anything like the girls in Molly's magazine. She wore baggy khaki shorts and a striped T-shirt and a red baseball cap on top of her curly black hair. She had big round glasses and freckles all over her face and arms. And worst of all, she wasn't wearing any makeup. Not even lipstick.

"Hi, Emily." Phyllis gave her a little hug.

"I'm so glad to meet you." She smelled of a kind of soap or perfume Emily had never smelled before.

"Hi," Emily mumbled, feeling shy.

Tom put his arm around Phyllis and squeezed her. "What do you think of my bride, Em? Isn't she something?"

Emily didn't know what to say.

"I've heard so much about you," Phyllis said. "Your pictures don't do you justice."

It sounded like a compliment.

"It's hot standing here in the sun," Tom said. "Sweetie, let's go over there and visit."

Emily thought he meant *her*. He always called her "sweetie." But instead he took Phyllis's hand and led the way to the clearing under the trees.

Emily trailed along beside them and sat down on a metal garden chair with a thump. "Why didn't you wait for me?" she exploded angrily.

"What do you mean?" Tom said.

"The wedding. Why did you have it without me?" Tears stung her eyes and she hoped she wouldn't cry.

Tom and Phyllis gave each other a look.

"Honey, there isn't time to explain it now," Tom said. "We can only stay for a little while. We'll tell you more about it when you come home."

"I wanted to be the flower girl," Emily said. "You promised."

"I did?" Tom looked confused.

"Here, I brought you this." Phyllis reached into her shorts pocket and pulled out a small package.

Slowly Emily took it and tore off the bow and tissue-paper wrapping. Inside was a ceramic duck pin.

"It's what all the girls are wearing," Phyllis said brightly.

"Well, *I'm* not!" Emily threw the pin on the ground. "It's for babies."

"Emily, pick that up," Tom scolded, "and thank Phyllis!"

"No," Emily said firmly, her arms folded across her chest.

Tom glared back at her. "You know, you're acting like a spoiled brat. What's gotten into you?"

"It's OK." Phyllis touched Tom's arm. "Forget it." She bent down to pick up the pin.

"No, don't." Tom scooped it up, dusted it off, and set it on the arm of his chair. "She has no right to treat you like that."

Tears filled Emily's eyes. Her brother had never raised his voice to her before, not even the time she accidentally broke one of his best records, an old one that he said couldn't be replaced.

"Look at our rings." Phyllis held out her hand. "Do you like them? Your dad got them for us."

Emily pretended not to care. "He gets *all* our jewelry," she said haughtily.

Sometimes Daddy would take her to his shop and let her sit at his workbench where he fixed broken watches and bracelets. Then he would clean her birthstone ring by dipping it in the saucepan of stuff cooking on the stove and drying it with a soft cloth until it shone.

"Daddy got *this* for me," Emily said, reaching under her T-shirt and pulling out her heart-shaped locket, "and when I learn to tell time he's going to get me a watch like his with a big hand, and a little hand, and numbers that go round in a circle."

Phyllis leaned forward and examined the locket. "Pretty. Does it open?"

Emily unfastened the catch and showed Phyllis the picture of Tom inside.

"I guess we have the same taste in men." Phyllis grinned. "I'm so lucky to have met your brother."

"I'm the lucky one," he said, rubbing the back of her neck. He kissed the tip of her nose, then her lips.

Phyllis kissed him back.

Emily was shocked. She had never seen her brother kiss a girl before. Suddenly he was a stranger to her. She rocked back and forth on her chair, not knowing what to do, where to look.

Overhead the leaves rustled as the wind blew through the trees. The sun flashed through the swaying branches. It was too bright. Looking into it made her squint and feel dizzy, like the time she nearly passed out playing volleyball on a very hot day. She wanted to be back on the playing field with the other kids doing relay races. Away from here. Away from Tom and Phyllis.

When she looked at them again dark spots danced in front of her eyes. They had stopped kissing and were asking her questions about camp. Before she knew it she was telling them about Molly and Paula and color war and being chosen captain of the green team for her cabin.

"Em," Tom said a little while later while she was right in the middle of a story about the Renaissance Fair and how she and Molly had run the lemonade stand, "we really have to get going."

"What do you mean, get going?" It seemed to Emily that they had just arrived.

Tom checked his watch and stood up. "We want to get to the lodge before it gets dark."

"But I didn't tell you about my costume."

Phyllis put her arm around her. "When you get home from camp you can come over to our apartment and tell me more about it. We'll have more time then."

Emily pulled away. If they really loved her they would stay longer and meet her friends. See her cabin. Sign her Snoopy autograph hound.

As they walked to the car Phyllis said, "Emily, I hope we'll be friends. I always wanted a sister and now I have one."

A sister. Clothes. Hand-me-downs. Someone to teach her how to set her hair the way Molly's sister had taught her.

Emily thought of what Molly had told her

and blurted out, "Are you going to have a baby?"

Tom chuckled.

Phyllis laughed. "Not for a long time. Some-day. Tom told me how you adore babies."

"I love babies." Emily remembered how it felt to hold her little cousin Daniel and give him his bottle. Tom and Phyllis's baby would belong to her even more. She would be the aunt. But they would be the mommy and daddy. Maybe Molly was right. Maybe they *were* going to do those disgusting things.

She studied them. No. Not Tom. Impos-sible. At least not with a girl like Phyllis. Why, she wasn't even wearing nail polish.

Emily held herself stiffly as Tom and Phyllis kissed her good-bye. Without waiting to see them off she turned and walked toward the dining hall where the kids were beginning to line up for lunch.

At her table Molly said, "Well, how was she?"

"Stupid."

"Is she pretty?"

Emily shook her head. "She wears big glasses and has ears that stick out."

"Ugh." Molly made a face. "Was she nice?"

Emily thought of the duck pin lying on the arm of the chair. It was kind of cute. She almost wanted to run outside and get it before somebody else found it. Finders, keepers, losers, weepers. Deep down she knew she had acted badly. This was one time she hadn't been Mommy's special girl, "good as gold." But Tom and Phyllis deserved it. They had had the wedding without her and she would never forgive them.

Never.

3

/|\\||\\||\\|

THE DAY AFTER EMILY GOT HOME FROM CAMP
her mother said they were going over to Tom
and Phyllis's for a visit.

"I don't want to go," Emily said.

"Don't you want to see their apartment? It's
so close we can walk. They were so lucky to
get something near us in Washington Heights.
The same thing downtown would be much
more expensive."

"I don't care."

"Emily, we're going and that's final."

They rode the elevator down to the lobby
of their apartment building and went out the
side entrance. Emily held her mother's hand
the way she always did outside, and they
started to walk uphill. It was a hot day. Emily's
shirt clung to her sweaty back. The air was so

thick she could hardly breathe. When they reached the park at the top of the hill she stopped to catch her breath.

"I want to go on the swings," she said, pulling away.

"Not now." At the corner her mother waited for the traffic light to change and led her across 181st Street.

Emily glanced at the doors leading to the subway station. "Can we ride the elevator down to the train?" she said.

"We don't need the train today. We can walk where we're going." Her mother marched her downhill toward the bakery, video store, and shoe store where she had bought her new saddle shoes that morning. Her mother had wanted her to pick shoes with Velcro fasteners but Emily knew how to tie laces. Tom had taught her when she was eight.

"Do you want to stop and get Tom and Phyllis a little gift?" her mother asked.

"No."

Her mother's eyebrows went up. "Are you sure? Maybe you'd like me to get something for you."

"No! I don't want to get them anything."

Her mother sighed deeply. "Emily, don't be difficult. Not today. It's too hot for a tantrum."

When they passed the Stork Baby Shop Emily let go of her mother's hand and ran to the window to see the display of cribs, carriages, and baby clothes. "Let's go in," she begged.

"We don't have time," her mother said.

"But you said we could stop for a gift."

"I don't like you going into that store."

"Why?"

"Emily, don't argue. We'll be late."

"Please? I want to talk to Hannah." Through the window Emily saw the young woman who owned the store and waved to her. Hannah waved back although she was talking to a customer. She always invited Emily to come in and look around. Once she let her push a stroller and showed her how it folded up.

"Come on, Emily." Her mother took her hand and led her away. In silence they walked the last few blocks up another hill to Tom and Phyllis's building. It was old and ugly. There was no lobby and no elevator. They climbed two flights of stairs and went down the hall to the apartment.

It was Phyllis who opened the door. She

was wearing jeans and the same striped T-shirt.

"Is that the only shirt you have?" Emily asked.

Her mother gave her a poke and kissed Phyllis.

"I was just writing thank-you notes." Phyllis showed them into the living room.

"Did you get any new things?" Emily's mother asked eagerly.

"Pink lace placemats." Phyllis rolled her eyes. "Wait'll you see them."

They were in a white box on the dining table. Emily picked one up and ran her finger along the edge. "They're beautiful."

"Emily, are your hands washed?" her mother asked.

Emily didn't bother answering. "Where's Tom?" She looked around.

Phyllis seemed surprised. "At work. It's Wednesday."

Emily's mother took Phyllis's arm and said in a low voice, "Emily has trouble remembering time."

"Don't say that!" Emily yelled. "I hardly make mistakes anymore." She felt like kicking her mother. Her elbow got itchy the way it did that time she got all dressed for school and it turned out to be a day Daddy was home.

"Honey, it's Sunday," he had said.

Now when he kissed her good-night he told her what the next day would be. At school all the kids had trouble with time but at least she knew that when the two hands were on the twelve it was time for lunch.

"Emily, stop scratching," her mother said.

Emily scratched anyway.

Phyllis said, "Anyone can make a mistake."

"I'd better get going," Emily's mother said, "and give you two a chance to get acquainted."

"I don't want to get acquainted." Emily followed her mother to the door.

"Be good, Emily." Her mother patted her cheek. "Mind Phyllis."

"Stop treating me like a baby!"

"Don't worry about a thing," Phyllis said. "We'll get along just fine."

After the door closed Phyllis said, "Want a tour of the apartment?" She opened the folding doors on one side of the living room. "*This* is the kitchen."

Emily gasped. There, like magic, were a

small stove, refrigerator, and sink. Phyllis took Emily's hand and showed her the bathroom and then the bedroom.

"Where's your wedding dress?" Emily asked, still feeling angry.

Phyllis opened the closet and unzipped a garment bag. She took out a dress. It was dark blue.

"Your *wedding* dress," Emily repeated.

"This *is* my wedding dress."

"But wedding dresses are long and white."

Phyllis snorted. "Not mine. I wouldn't be caught dead in one of those jobs."

Emily scratched her elbow. "Wedding dresses are always white. I've seen them on TV."

Her favorite episode of *The Brady Bunch* was the one where Mr. and Mrs. Brady got married with her daughters as bridesmaids and his sons as best men. Every time Emily saw it she got goose bumps and tears came to her eyes. Then she'd laugh out loud when the dog knocked over the wedding cake and Mr. Brady caught it. Sure he got mad and threw cake at Mrs. Brady but at the end of the show they kissed and made up. They always did. That's how weddings were supposed to be.

To Phyllis she said, "At weddings there's a big party and lots of dancing and a tall cake and . . ."

"Emily," Phyllis interrupted, "did you think we had a big wedding without you?"

Emily nodded, looking at the floor. A lump formed in her throat.

Phyllis put her arm around her shoulders. "Oh, honey, we'd never do that. It was just a simple ceremony in the judge's office. Your folks, my dad and his wife. Then lunch at a hotel. Even my own mother didn't come."

"She didn't?" Now Emily was really confused.

But Phyllis didn't explain. She laughed. "You should have seen me. I didn't wear my glasses. Everything was a blur. Tom had to lead me around."

As Emily listened to the details she felt the hard knot of anger beginning to loosen and by the time Phyllis showed her her wedding hat, Emily was ready to see all her clothes. Her shoes were lined up in rows.

"I like those." Emily pointed to a pair of red high heels with lots of straps.

Phyllis picked them up. "They hurt my feet. Would you like to try them on?"

Emily's heart fluttered. She had never tried on a pair of shoes like those before, not even at the shoe store. Her mother and father thought she was too young for heels. Emily took off her brand-new saddle shoes and socks and stepped into the delicate sandals. They were a little too big. The strap around the heel was loose.

Phyllis smiled. "You look great." She opened her dresser drawer and pulled out a big black shawl and wrapped it around Emily. From the closet she took out a straw hat with an upturned brim. She piled Emily's dark brown hair on top of her head and tucked it under the hat. "Look at yourself," she said.

Emily wobbled to the dresser and gazed at herself in the mirror. She was gorgeous! Like one of the girls in Molly's magazine. Like Marcia Brady on TV. She looked again to make sure. "Phyllis," she asked, "do you think I look blank?"

"Of course not. Who told you that?"

"Someone."

She knew she didn't look thirteen. Cheryl and Amanda who lived in her building were thirteen. They were best friends. Every morning she would see them while she waited for her school bus. They wore dangle earrings, lipstick, eye makeup, miniskirts, and lace-up boots with little heels and pointy toes. They'd show off and talk extra loud to teenage boys like Patrick Duggan who lived down the block. They'd say funny things to each other and laugh but when they saw her they'd say, "Hello, Emily. How are you, Emily?" as if she were a baby. If only they could see her now.

She picked up a perfume bottle and smelled it. It was the same sweet scent Phyllis had worn the day she visited at camp.

"Like it?" Phyllis sprayed some on Emily's neck. She put a black velvet hat on her own head and took Emily's hand. "We're two ladies going to tea at the Palm Court."

Emily giggled. This was more fun than playing dress-up at school. Hand in hand she and Phyllis walked to the other side of the bed and sat down.

"Wait a minute. We need jewelry." Phyllis went to the dresser and brought back a box. "For you," she said, taking out a bead necklace with hearts and cows dangling from it.

Emily remembered the ceramic duck pin

Phyllis had given her at camp. She was glad she had gone back that day to get it.

Phyllis fastened the beads around Emily's neck and slipped some silver bracelets on her arm. "Lovely weather we're having," she said in a funny voice and pretended to drink a cup of tea. Then she pulled her glasses down her nose and peered over them at Emily. "My dear, what a charming hat you're wearing! Wherever did you get it?"

"You," Emily laughed.

"Do tell," Phyllis said in the same funny voice. She held her hand to her ear. "I say, they're playing a waltz. May I have this dance, Madam?" She stood up, took Emily's hand, and danced her around the bedroom.

"Not so fast." Emily tried to keep her balance and hold on to her hat, but Phyllis wouldn't slow down.

She hummed some music and spun Emily around the room.

"My hat!" Emily yelled as it fell off. She shrieked and laughed and Phyllis laughed with her.

Suddenly there was a loud thumping. They stopped dancing.

"Uh-oh," Phyllis said in her regular voice. "That's Mrs. Shoeman downstairs, the old biddy. She's always banging on the ceiling with her broom."

There was more thumping.

"All right, all right, you old witch," Phyllis said as they collapsed on the bed. "Save your broom for flying."

Emily stretched out on the blue-and-white striped comforter. "Phyllis, is this your bed?"

"Yes. Tom's too."

Emily didn't understand. At home Tom slept in his own bed like her. Aloud she said, "Where does he put on his pajamas?"

"Right here."

"Where do you put on yours?"

"Here."

"My mommy *never* lets me get undressed in front of Tom. I'm never allowed out of my bedroom without clothes on."

"It's different when you're married. Married people see each other without clothes on."

"Why?"

"Part of loving somebody is knowing everything about them."

Emily laughed. "Even seeing them naked?"

Phyllis's face got red. "Emily, don't you know that when people get married . . . they sleep together? . . . like your mommy and daddy." All of a sudden she jumped up and put her hat away in the closet.

Emily felt like kicking herself. She knew she had said something wrong. It was like the time she had burst into Mommy and Daddy's bedroom to show them her food scrapbook and they were in bed under the covers. When she asked what they were doing her daddy had pretended he was asleep and her mommy had said in a scolding voice, "Taking a nap. Now, Emily, next time please knock."

There were so many rules to remember. Sometimes she couldn't remember them all and cried. Then they'd say she was being a crybaby. I'll never cry in front of Phyllis, she promised herself. I'll try to be good.

But Phyllis didn't seem mad. She said, "I'll show you my other jewelry," and dumped her box of earrings on the bed. They looked at every pair.

Emily loved looking at jewelry. Sometimes when her daddy came home from his shop he'd unlock his big brown bag and show her the

customers' rings and watches, each in a sepa-
rate envelope. Once he had taken a folded tissue out of one of the envelopes. Inside were
tiny sparkling stones. "These are diamonds,"
he had said. "They're precious, like you."

She knew that was good because of the way
he said it.

Phyllis tapped the star earrings in her ears.
"I like these the best. Your brother gave them
to me."

"How do you get them in and out?" Emily
asked.

Phyllis took one off and showed her.

Emily stared, open-mouthed. "Does it
hurt?"

"No. I've had pierced ears since I was a
baby. If I ever have a little girl I'll have her
ears pierced when she's born."

Emily thought of the things Molly had told
her. *And pretty soon they'll have a baby.* She
thought of the other things Molly had whispered. This was her chance to find out for sure.
Again she blurted out, "Phyllis, when will you
and Tom have a baby?"

"Maybe someday when I finish school."
Phyllis put the earrings back in the box.

"You go to school?"

"A kind of school called college."

It was almost funny. Why would Phyllis bother to go to school when she could stay home in her own apartment and look at her jewelry and try on her clothes and have a baby?

"I want a baby," she told Phyllis.

At first Phyllis didn't say anything. "Emily, people usually get married before they have babies."

"I don't want to get married. I just want to have a baby." It would be hers. She and the baby would love each other and spend every day together.

"Emily," Phyllis said, "do you know how babies are made?"

"Sure."

"Tell me."

Emily traced a blue stripe on the comforter with her finger. "I know you have to take your top off."

"That's right. Remember we talked about loving someone and knowing everything about them? But there's more."

There's more. That's what Molly had said. Emily's stomach tightened. "Like what?"

"When you want a baby you kiss very long, and get the closest you can get—"

"How long?" Emily interrupted.

"The loving and kissing can be for a little while or a long while, but it takes nine months for the baby to grow."

"We're learning months at school," Emily said, "January, February, May . . ."

"Come on." Phyllis pulled Emily to her feet. "I'm starving. Let's get something to eat."

Over Diet Coke, grapes and Raspberry Newtons, Phyllis's favorite cookie, Phyllis told Emily about her romance with Tom and how they had met and married in less than four weeks. Then she told about her mother and father and how they got divorced. Although Emily didn't understand much of it she enjoyed listening. Phyllis made her feel older, more grown-up.

When it was time for her to go home with her mother she threw her arms around Phyllis's neck and wouldn't let go.

At the door Phyllis said, "Emily, call me whenever you want to."

"I don't know your number."

"Wait. I'll write it down for you." She went into the bedroom and came back with a slip of paper.

Emily held it tightly in her hand on the way home. The sweat from her palm blurred the pencil marks a little but she could still read the numbers when she put the paper on her nightstand.

Before dinner she walked into the living room. The windows were wide open and the fan on the little table was going full blast. Her father was sitting in his big green chair. His bare feet rested on the footrest that pushed out. His chair was the biggest in the living room. It faced the couch on one side, and the TV in the corner. But he wasn't watching TV now. He was reading the newspaper. Some of the sections lay scattered on the floor beside his chair.

"I want pierced ears," Emily said.

Her father looked up from his paper. "Where did you get that idea?"

"From my sister-in-law." Just saying the word made her feel powerful.

"You might get an infection," her mother called from the kitchen.

Her father turned a page. "What do you need earrings for at your age?"

"I want to look pretty like Phyllis."

"I'll bring you all the earrings you want," her father said. "The kind that clip on, like Mommy's."

"I want pierced ears like Phyllis."

Her mother came into the living room wearing a mitt and carrying a cooking spoon. "Let's discuss it another time."

"I don't want to wear these shoes anymore," Emily added, scuffing the white parts on purpose.

"But those are the ones you wanted this morning," her mother said.

"I don't want them now."

Her father put down his paper. "Hold on. You just got those today. They cost a bundle."

"I don't like them. They're baby shoes."

"Emily," her mother said, "why don't you water the plants. Have you forgotten?"

"You know I never forget!" Emily shouted at her mother. She ran into the kitchen and got the watering can from the cupboard beneath the sink. While she turned on the faucet she heard her father say, "What's the matter with her?"

"Forget it, Irv," was her mother's answer.

I won't forget, Emily promised herself. I'm going to be just like Phyllis.

4

WHEN SCHOOL STARTED EMILY FELT LIKE PHYL-
lis as she learned how to use the new washing
machine and dryer in her classroom. Her
teacher, Mr. Davis, showed all the students
how to put in a load of towels and tablecloths,
pour out the right amount of Tide into a cup,
and add it to the wash.

"We have to learn how to take care of our-
selves," he said, "and stay neat and clean."

Emily poured the Tide without spilling a
drop, trickled it into the machine and closed
the lid. She stared at the panel of buttons and
couldn't remember which ones to push.

"Teacher, I need help," she said, raising her
hand. I always need help, she scolded herself.
Would Mr. Davis laugh at her?

"Emily, you asked in a nice way," he said.
"Donny, please show her how to do it."

Donny came over to the washing machine, pushed the buttons and said, "Turn the dial this way."

Emily spun the dial.

"Now pull it out," Donny said.

Emily tugged at the dial and the machine started to hum. She could hear the water running in. "Thanks, Donny." She smiled.

He was taller than she was and always wore a clean shirt to school. Not a T-shirt with a brand name or funny picture like the kind the other boys wore, but a shirt with buttons and a collar. And he wore it tucked into his pants. His straight blond hair was cut short and combed into place.

"I have a new watch," Donny said, "and it doesn't matter if it gets wet."

She loked at the numbers and the black strap. It was a watch like her father's. She could see the blond hairs on Donny's wrist. "I have something new too."

"What?"

"Guess." Emily giggled.

"Is it a watch?"

"No. It's much bigger."

"Is it a bike?"

She laughed and shook her head. "It's a sister and I'm going to her house for dinner tonight."

Later, on the way home in the school bus, Emily began to worry about the dinner. What if she laughed in the wrong place when her father told a joke? What if she couldn't cut her meat by herself? What if she dropped food on the floor or broke one of Tom and Phyllis's new wedding dishes? Phyllis might get angry and not like her anymore.

When the bus dropped her off at her building, she hurried upstairs to change. "I want to get them a present," she said to her mother.

"Now?" Her mother zipped up the back of Emily's jumper, straightened the collar of her blouse and pinned on her ceramic duck pin. She helped her into her gray cardigan sweater. "We don't have time. You told Phyllis you'd come over early and help her shop and cook."

Emily emptied her silver chick bank on her bed and spread out the money. "Is this enough?"

Her mother sighed. "You're going to spend all that? I thought you were saving for a tape."

"Mommy, it's for *them!*" She stuffed the

coins in her jumper pockets until they bulged. Her pockets jingled with every step she took all the way to the store.

The florist's, across the street from the Stork Baby Shop, was another one of Emily's favorite places, because of the smell. She strolled around the store looking at all the flowers, sniffing their delicious fragrances.

"Need some help?" the florist asked Emily's mother.

"My daughter's choosing a gift."

"How about some mums?" He pulled a bouquet of rust-colored ones out of a tall vase and bunched them with orange and gold leaves. "It makes a lovely fall display."

Emily shook her head.

"Would you like some roses? We're having a special sale." He slid open a glass case and a blast of cold air hit Emily. She gazed longingly at the deep red and pale pink buds. They were beautiful but she knew they wouldn't last.

"Come on, dear," her mother said. "We don't have all day."

"How much does she want to spend?" the florist asked Emily's mother.

Emily took a handful of coins out of the

pocket of her plaid jumper and showed him.

"For $4.29 she could get a nice little planter." He picked up a basket with different kinds of plants and a ceramic frog in the middle.

"It's for my brother and sister-in-law," Emily explained.

"Emily, make up your mind now or we'll come back another time," her mother said impatiently.

"Mommy, don't rush me." Emily scratched her elbow through her sweater. She needed time to make a good choice. She wanted this gift to be wonderful, something they would adore. All at once she saw what she wanted. "That one." She pointed to a violet plant with tiny purple flowers. It was wrapped in pink and white cellophane that looked like lace.

"How much?" Emily's mother said.

"Four-fifty."

Emily dumped all her money on the counter and watched as her mother and the florist counted out the right amount.

"What color ribbon?" the florist asked Emily's mother.

"It's Emily's gift."

"Blue," she said, remembering it was Phyllis's favorite color.

Feeling proud, she carried the plant to Tom and Phyllis's apartment. She could hardly wait to give it to them. In her mind she pictured how pleased they'd be to receive it.

When Phyllis opened the door Emily said, "This is for you. It's a wedding present."

"Emily bought it with her own money," her mother added.

"It's beautiful. Thanks, honey." Phyllis kissed Emily and took the plant. She put it in the middle of the dining table. "I'll take good care of it. You'll have to tell me how often to water it. Tom says you know all about that stuff."

Emily glowed. She had done something right for once.

" 'Bye, girls," Emily's mother said. "I'll do a few errands and meet you back here around six."

As soon as the door closed Emily squealed with joy. She and Phyllis were alone, sisters together. "What are we having for dinner?" she asked.

"Marinated chicken breasts, rice pilaf with almonds and raisins . . ."

Although Emily didn't know what all those things were, her mouth watered. She loved talking about food and thinking about what she'd eat.

"At school we cut out pictures of food from magazines," she said. "And we bake cakes and make picnic sandwiches. I work in the cafeteria with Mrs. T."

"Who's she?" Phyllis asked.

"The cook. She calls me her little scooper." Emily giggled. "I dish up lunches and put out snacks."

"I'm splurging tonight," Phyllis said. "We're even going to have baby vegetables."

Emily hung on the word baby as they took the bright blue shopping cart out of the hall closet and set out for Daitch's Shopwell. On the way she held Phyllis's hand the way she always held her mother's. If she got lost she'd never find her way home again. Just thinking about it made her heart pound in terror.

Yesterday Donny told how he had gotten lost. He had done what their teacher, Mr. Davis, had taught them to do—he had gone to a pay phone and called his aunt. Emily thought he was very smart to do that.

When Mr. Davis asked what else they could

do if they were lost some of the kids shouted, "Ask a policeman," and "Ask someone on the street," but Emily couldn't think of anything. She listened carefully when Mr. Davis told them again to look for a bank or a post office and go in and ask for help.

Now as the light turned green and the WALK sign flashed on, she and Phyllis hurried across 181st Street to Daitch Shopwell on the other side.

Emily took a deep breath. The crowded market full of clanging carts and people bumping into each other mixed her up. Inside, Phyllis grabbed a shopping cart and gave it to Emily to push. Emily weaved down the aisle, skillfully steering the cart past a display of back-to-school lunch boxes while Phyllis walked alongside her, pulling the blue cart and studying her list.

"We need olive oil, onions, boneless chicken breasts . . ."

At the meat section Emily held onto the cart and stayed close to Phyllis. She didn't touch anything, the way her mother had taught her. If she was good as gold Phyllis would like her even more.

From the corner of her eye Emily noticed two little boys at the bakery counter staring at her. People often stared—in restaurants, movie theaters, department stores. The best thing to do was ignore them or stare back, the way Molly did.

Once, at camp, when they had hiked to the Grey House for brownie sundaes some ladies at the next table had stared at them and whispered words like "retarded" and "strange" and "too bad." Lately Emily had begun to notice they *did* look different from other people, especially the fat kids with mismatched clothes and odd, unbecoming haircuts.

Not Molly, though. She had turned around and shouted at the ladies, "What are you looking at, huh? Are you retarded or something?"

Emily and the other kids had burst out laughing as the ladies pretended to be busy talking to each other. That Molly! She sure knew how to fix them. If only she were here now to help her say something to make the boys go away.

Phyllis was carefully selecting a package of chicken. "Emily," she said, "would you please get a jar of dill pickles? D-I-L-L. It's the big jar with the square red label, right behind you."

Emily let go of the cart and slowly circled around. The boys were watching her and snickering. One of them whispered something to the other.

She knew they were telling secrets about her. Her stomach hurt as though she had been punched. She tried not to pay attention and studied the pickles. There were so many kinds—fat ones, skinny ones, sliced ones. Where were the ones Phyllis wanted? Her head swam as she searched the rows.

"Look at that weird kid," one of the boys said loudly. "Hey, how old are you, kid? What school do you go to?"

Emily held back tears. She spotted dill pickles with a square red label and quickly reached for the jar.

"She's a re-tard," the other boy shouted. "Re-tard!"

Emily burst into tears. "Stupid!" she shouted back. "You big stupid!"

The jar slid from her hand and fell to the floor with a smash. She let out a scream and backed up and banged into the whole section of pickles. There was a loud crash and suddenly the floor was covered with pickles, broken glass and pickle juice. Juice splashed her shoes and socks.

Phyllis spun around. "Emily, what happened? Are you all right?"

The boys laughed. "What a geek."

"Hey, dummy! Toss me a pickle!"

A voice on the loudspeaker said, "Courtesy clerk. Wet cleanup on aisle number 15A."

Everyone was looking at her. *Everyone.* Emily wished she were home. She wished she were at Camp Pleasant Lake. She wished she were at school where kids had accidents all the time and no one made fun of them. Sobbing, her nose running, she covered her eyes with her hands to hide from Phyllis.

Phyllis put her arm around her and patted her back. She wiped Emily's face with a Kleenex. "Take it easy, Em. It could happen to anyone."

Emily knew it couldn't. It would never happen to Cheryl and Amanda. Phyllis was probably sorry she had brought her to the market. She was probably sorry she got Emily for a sister-in-law in the first place.

The boys were still watching.

"Buzz off, you jerks!" Phyllis scowled. "Beat it!"

The boys turned and ran.

"Creeps!" Phyllis called after them.

"Creeps!" Emily echoed. It cheered her up a little to call them names.

"Come on." Phyllis gave Emily the blue cart. With one hand she pushed the big shopping cart and with the other she took Emily's hand and they sidestepped glass and pickles. A teenaged boy in a shop apron came toward them carrying a broom, trash basket, mop and pail.

Emily felt awful as Phyllis led the way to the manager's station.

"I'm very sorry about our little accident," Phyllis said.

"Are you hurt?" the manager asked Emily. He wore a bow tie and badge.

She shook her head.

"We're OK," Phyllis said.

Emily liked the way she said "we."

"If you break it you buy it," the manager said. "That's store policy."

"How much do we owe you?" Phyllis said crisply.

"Well, a few jars of pickles . . . let's say five bucks and we'll call it even." The manager wrote something on a piece of paper and handed it to Phyllis. "Give this to the clerk when you check out."

Phyllis took Emily's hand again and marched her to the cookie section where she found a package of Raspberry Newtons. To Emily's amazement she ripped open the wrapper and they ate cookies right there in the market. Then they paid the bill and left.

Back at the apartment Phyllis cooked dinner while Emily set the table.

"How many people?" Emily asked.

"Five." Phyllis gave Emily a bunch of blue-and-white–checked cloth napkins. "This is the only pattern we have more than four of."

Emily counted out loud as she put a napkin at each place on the table. "One for Mommy, one for Daddy, one for Tom . . ." Her wedding present plant looked pretty. She felt the dirt in the pot to see if it needed water.

Phyllis wiped wineglasses with a dish towel and set them out. "Tonight's a special occasion."

"What do you mean?"

"It's a secret. I can't tell you till Tom comes home."

When his key sounded in the lock they both ran to the door to greet him. He kissed Phyllis first. Emily couldn't look.

Then he put down his briefcase and with an arm around each of their waists he said, "How are my girls?"

"Something terrible happened at the market," Emily said.

"What?"

"Some boys called me re-tard and I dropped the pickles."

Tom's face darkened and he said a bad word. He called the boys a name Emily's mother had told her never to use. "I'd like to wring their necks." Tom ruffled Emily's hair. "I'm sorry, honey."

"I'm OK," she said, smoothing her hair in place.

When her parents arrived she felt more like a hostess than a guest. Phyllis let her pass the

tray of cheese and crackers around and, after
drinks, put the salad and salad plates on the
table. Tom poured wine for the grown-ups
except Phyllis. He gave her fizzy water and
Emily a Diet Coke.

Before they began eating Tom said, "Phyllis
and I have something to tell you." He turned
to Phyllis. Her eyes sparkled through her
glasses. Her cheeks were pink. There was a
smile on her lips. "We're going to have a baby,"
he said.

Shivers ran down Emily's spine.

"A baby!" Her mother looked like she was
going to cry. "When?"

"End of April, beginning of May," Phyllis
said.

"We're going to be grandparents!" Emily's
father leapt up and loudly kissed Tom and
Phyllis both.

Emily couldn't move.

Her mother rushed over to Phyllis and gave
her a hug. "Do you feel all right? Have you
seen a doctor? What about school?"

Tom laughed. "Ma, take it easy."

Emily's father said, "Isabelle, sit down and
relax."

"We didn't plan it this way," Phyllis said, "but I'll still be able to go to school. Maybe they'll let me finish early."

Tom put his arm around her and kissed her hair. "Little mother."

She snuggled against him.

They looked at Emily. "What do you think, Em? You're going to be an aunt."

Emily was too embarrassed to answer them. It couldn't be true. It couldn't. She pushed away her salad plate and wrung her checkered napkin in her hands. Tom and her parents seemed far away as they fussed over Phyllis, happily showing off a new ring Tom had given her. For Emily the party was over. She had never felt so disgusted in her whole life.

Her father raised his glass and made a toast. "To the new baby."

Emily took a sip of her Diet Coke and turned over in her mind the things Molly had told her and whispered. So Phyllis had really taken off her top in front of Tom. And Tom had taken off his pants in front of Phyllis. And they slept in the same bed. And then . . . And then . . . *When you want a baby you kiss very long and get the closest you can get*, Phyllis had said. Up till now Emily hadn't really believed her. She had put the idea out of her mind. Besides, Phyllis had said she and Tom wouldn't have a baby for a long while. So surely they wouldn't have done those terrible things.

5

//|||\\\

AFTER THE DINNER PARTY EMILY DIDN'T WANT
to see Phyllis anymore. Once when Phyllis and
Tom came over Emily stayed in her room the
whole time, playing with her postcard collec-
tion. The museum card that used to be her
favorite, showing a lady in a gown holding a
chubby naked baby, suddenly looked ugly.
She tore it up and threw the pieces into her
wastebasket. Phyllis knocked on the door and
asked to come in and look at postcards with
her but Emily pretended she was getting ready
for bed.

Another time when her mother went over
to see their new rocking chair Emily said
she didn't want to go and went to the shop
with her father instead and watched him fix
jewelry.

But after a few weeks Emily began to miss Phyllis and hoped she would call. She didn't, and it was getting close to Halloween.

One day Emily found the piece of paper with Phyllis's phone number and called her. "Phyllis? It's me, Emily."

"How are you, honey?" Phyllis yawned. "What's up?"

"I don't know what to be for Halloween. We're having a parade at school and I have to wear a costume."

"How about going as a ghost?"

"I was a ghost last time."

Phyllis yawned again. "A princess? You could wear a crown."

"I don't have a crown."

"Look, Em. I'm too tired to talk about it now."

Emily looked out her window. There was still daylight. Why was Phyllis so sleepy?

"I saw some neat costumes at Sav-On," Phyllis said. "Maybe your mom could take you there." She hung up and Emily wondered whether she was angry with her for staying away for so long.

Phyllis didn't seem to want to be close to

Emily the way she had when she and Tom
were first married. There were no more invi-
tations to come over and try on hats and shoes
and play going for tea at the Palm Court.

Phyllis didn't like her anymore. Maybe she
would never feel the same way about her now
that she was going to have a baby. It seemed
that was all she could talk about. Once when
she came over for dinner right after Halloween
she wore Tom's shirt with the tails hanging
out. Emily thought she looked sloppy but she
explained she couldn't zip up her jeans, and
Emily's mother made a plan to take her shopping that Saturday.

While they were gone Emily stayed with
Tom and helped him vacuum the apartment
and make macaroni salad for lunch. It was her
job to cut up the celery.

"Just think, Em, you're going to be an aunt."
Tom squeezed lemon juice on the cooled macaroni and sprinkled it with salt.

"I know," she said.

"You don't seem real excited. I thought you
loved babies so much."

"I do, but . . ." This was her chance. She
wanted to ask Tom if Phyllis had to take her

top off in front of him to have the baby but was too shy to say it out loud.

"What do you think it will be," he asked her, "a boy or a girl?"

Emily shrugged and dumped the celery into the bowl of macaroni. Tom added mayonnaise, then mixed the whole thing together with his hands the way he always did and gave her a spoonful to taste. "Enough lemon?"

Emily smacked her lips and nodded. She loved Tom's cooking. He knew how to make a lot of good things—hamburgers, fruit salad, and scrambled eggs just the way she liked them. He could even mix two kinds of Campbell's soup together to make a new soup.

If only they were having lunch alone, the two of them, the way they used to before Tom was married! They'd listen to the radio or a tape while they were eating, and afterward play with the electric trains. Or Tom would read and Emily would draw pictures.

Now the front door opened and Emily's mother called gaily, "Wait till you see what we got! We bought out the whole store!"

Phyllis took off her coat. She was wearing one of her new outfits, a dark blue jumper with red buttons and a matching red print blouse.

"Pretty," Tom said.

Phyllis beamed. "I really look pregnant, don't I!"

Tom took her in his arms and kissed her.

"There's another blouse to go with it," Phyllis said, "and I can also wear your shirts underneath."

"Navy blue goes with everything," Emily's mother added.

Emily felt angry. They were too busy fussing over those new clothes to pay attention to her. That baby was changing things already and it wasn't even born yet. "When do we eat lunch?" she burst out.

"Now." They sat down at the table and Tom served Phyllis first but she didn't eat much.

"What's the matter?" Tom said. "Don't you like it?"

"I'm not hungry."

"I am." Emily held up her plate for more.

"You've got to eat," Tom urged Phyllis. "It's for the baby."

"The baby gets what it needs."

How? Emily wondered.

"Are you feeling OK?" Emily's mother asked Phyllis. "Maybe the shopping tired you out."

"I didn't sleep well last night." Phyllis pushed her glasses up and rubbed her eyes. "I kept having bad dreams."

I have bad dreams all the time and no one worries about me, Emily thought. Sometimes she'd dream she was lost downtown and didn't know how to get home. Once she woke up from a dream about riding on a bus along strange streets and got out of bed, not knowing where she was. She walked around her room touching chairs and doorknobs, bumping into walls, until slowly she remembered she was in her own room and went back to bed.

"Lie down and take a nap after lunch." Tom patted Phyllis's hand.

"Have you decided on names?" Emily's mother asked brightly.

"Luke for a boy," Tom said.

"Samantha for a girl," Phyllis said. "Maybe Sabrina."

Tom rolled his eyes. "I hope it's a boy."

Emily used to know exactly what she would name her baby. Janet. It would be a girl.

Maybe she could get it in a different way. Maybe the angels could bring it to her the way they brought the chubby baby to the lady in the painting. The guide at the art museum had told them all about it when the class took a field trip there.

"Just hope for a normal, healthy baby," Emily's mother said now.

Suddenly it was quiet. The only sound was Emily's fork scraping on her plate. They wanted to say something about how her head didn't work right. About learning disabilities. She knew it. They always got quiet when they wanted to talk about her and she was in the room.

Tom cleared his throat. "How about a cup of coffee?" he said to Phyllis. "That'll make you feel better."

"Tom, you know what the studies show. Too much caffeine during pregnancy can be harmful to the baby."

"There's no conclusive proof. How about a cup of tea, then?"

"Tea has caffeine, too. And we're out of herb tea."

"Phyllis, you worry too much." Tom stood up and cleared the dishes.

"Lie down and rest," Emily's mother said to Phyllis. "It'll do you good."

"Come and keep me company," she said.

Emily got up to follow them but her mother stopped her. "Stay here, dear."

"Why? I want to be with Phyllis."

"Emily, do as I say."

Emily knew that tone of voice. She went to the TV and turned it on while Tom washed the dishes. An ad for lipstick came on, and Emily remembered the last time she and Phyllis had done something together.

Phyllis had taken her to Bloomingdale's, the largest department store Emily had ever been in. There was so much to see it made her dizzy. What if she got lost or caught in the escalator? She held onto Phyllis's hand the whole time. In the cosmetics department they sat side by side on high stools trying on lipstick and eye-shadow. With each new layer Emily looked into the magnifying mirror, searching to see if the blank expression was gone.

When she said, "Phyllis, do you like this shade of lipstick on me?" Phyllis let out a shriek of laughter.

"Oh, Lord. Look at you!"

"Do I look blank?"

"No way. You look great."

Emily wanted to leave the makeup on for the rest of the day and maybe not wash it off that night, but Phyllis suggested she wipe off a little before they went home. If only she could go in the bedroom now and try on Phyllis's high heels and hats.

She flipped the dial of the TV set and found one of her favorite shows, "The Munsters." When a commercial came on about floor wax that started with a fight, she turned down the sound and heard her mother and Phyllis talking.

She could tell they were talking about something important. She heard her name and the words "developmental delay." She had heard those words before. They meant it took her longer to learn things than anybody else—even simple things like zipping a zipper, or buttoning buttons, or tying her shoelaces.

Emily tiptoed into the hallway and moved closer to the bedroom door. It was partly open.

Her mother was saying, "Are you worried about having a child who is retarded like Emily?"

They were using those words again. Emily's heart beat fast.

"Phyllis, just because Emily is the way she is doesn't mean your baby will be. It's generally due to heredity but in my case there was a decreased flow of oxygen during labor."

In a low voice Phyllis said something about tests and doctors.

Then Emily's mother said, "Maybe keeping her was selfish. I worry about what will happen when Irv and I are gone."

Phyllis said, "Listen, Isabelle, Tom and I are here. We'll always look after Emily. I know she won't be able to take care of herself."

What did Phyllis mean? Emily wanted to burst into the room and shout, I do *too* know how to take care of myself! I can get washed and dressed and tie my shoes and brush my hair! I can even give myself a shampoo!

She was almost mad at Phyllis but then she heard her say, "I really love Emily."

Emily peeked into the room. Phyllis was lying on the bed, her head propped against some pillows. Emily's mother sat next to her. She noticed Emily right away. "Emily, how long have you been standing there?" She and Phyllis exchanged looks. "Well, come on over here, darling, and join us."

Emily walked over to the bed and sat down

beside her mother. Phyllis rolled over to face them, her head resting on her arm.

Emily's mother gave her a hug and smoothed her bangs away from her forehead. "Phyllis, did you know this girl has special jobs at school?"

"Yes." Phyllis squeezed Emily's hand. "She told me about working in the cafeteria."

"I get stars," Emily said. "We trade our stars for prizes. I'm saving up for a perfume-bottle necklace."

"I've never seen one of those before," Phyllis said. "Will you show it to me when you get it?"

"Sure."

"You know, some of the children at Emily's school have severe learning disabilities," her mother said. "Only a few are as capable as Emily. She helps take care of the younger children. Her teachers have nothing but praise for her."

Emily rubbed her cheek against her mother's shoulder. She felt good when her mother said nice things about her.

"The baby's going to be lucky to have you for an aunt." Phyllis smiled.

"I love this girl," Emily's mother said, "and Phyllis, we're going to love your baby too."

"Will you love my baby?" Emily said.

"What baby?" Her mother frowned.

"The one the angels are going to bring me."

"*Angels!* Where did you hear that?" Her mother shot Phyllis a look.

"At the art museum."

"Emily," Phyllis said, "remember we talked about how babies are made?"

Emily nodded.

"Did you forget? Let me tell you again."

After Phyllis and her mother finished telling her, Emily was quiet. She wondered if Molly knew all this stuff too. She had said, "There's more." Is this what she had meant? Had Phyllis told Emily everything?

In a way Emily wished none of it was true. How could something as wonderful as a baby come from doing something like *that?* It was too awful to think about.

6

AT SCHOOL EMILY DECIDED TO WORK HARDER than ever at her jobs to earn stars. She needed one hundred for her perfume-bottle necklace.

One rainy Monday morning Emily went to Mrs. Polarski's room, her old room, to help with the eight- and nine-year-olds the way she did every day.

"I'm sure glad to see you." Mrs. Polarski sighed. "We had to stay in during recess because of the weather, and the children are restless. If you do a very good job I'll give you two bonus stars."

Emily tingled with excitement. "What do you want me to do?"

"Play with Wanda today. She's been causing problems. I think she needs some special attention."

"OK." Feeling confident and grown-up, Emily strode over to the toy stove.

Wanda was noisily banging it with a pan. Near her Victor and some of the kids playing supermarket yelled, "Be quiet!"

As soon as Wanda saw Emily she dropped her pan and hugged her.

Emily glowed. She was a real teacher. At the phonograph Yvonne waved hello. Yvonne had been a student at the school. Now she worked here as Mrs. Polarski's aide. She put on a record of "Three Blind Mice" and some of the children started dancing.

"Wanda," Emily said in Phyllis's take-charge tone of voice, "let's play house. I'll be the mommy and you be the baby."

Wanda put her thumb in her mouth.

"What do you want for dinner?"

Wanda took her thumb out of her mouth. "Man chops." Like many of the children at school she had trouble talking clearly, but Emily understood her anyway.

Emily opened the play refrigerator and took out toy meat. "What else do you want?"

"Peas and cawwots." Wanda grabbed a real

can of peas and carrots from the supermarket shelf and handed it to Emily.

"No, no." Emily put the can back on the shelf. "We're just playing."

Victor left the toy cash register and rushed over to hug Emily.

Wanda pushed him away and wrapped her arms around Emily. "*My* Emmy."

It felt good when the children fought over her, although she knew it was her job to help them play nicely. Luckily Victor skipped off to the dress-up corner, put on a fireman's hat, and galloped around the room.

"Victor, not so much noise," Mrs. Polarski called. "Let's work on our shoe tying." She went to the closet and took out the practice shoe.

Mimicking her, Emily picked up a baby doll. "Wanda, let's work on dressing the baby." Soon there'd be a real baby. Phyllis and Tom's. Would they let her hold it, give it a bottle, dress it? She found a hat and put it on the doll's head.

Wanda tried to tie the ribbons under the doll's chin. Emily sat down in one of the little chairs and watched her, remembering how she used to play with dolls when she was in this class.

Suddenly José ran over and snatched the doll from Wanda.

"Mine!" she screamed.

"I want it!" José kicked her.

Wanda burst into tears. Emily trembled. Teachers and helpers were supposed to stop fights but she didn't know how. She jumped up and tugged at the doll in José's arms, but he held on tightly and wouldn't let go. Now he was screaming too.

The racket made Emily dizzy. Her heart beat fast. She looked around feeling helpless, wondering what to do.

Yvonne stared at her.

Mrs. Polarski hurried over. "What's going on here?"

Wanda pointed to the doll. "Mine!"

José stuck his tongue out at her.

"Emily, I thought you were playing house with Wanda."

"I was. He came over and took the doll."

"OK, OK. José, it's Wanda's turn to have the doll." Mrs. Polarski simply took it from him and gave it back to Wanda. "Come on,

let's do some bead work." She took his hand
and led him to the table.

Wanda stopped crying and put the doll in
the carriage.

Emily sank into the little chair. Why
couldn't I do that, she asked herself. What's
the matter with me? She knew she had done
a bad job. Probably she wouldn't earn extra
stars. Maybe she'd earn none at all. Phyllis was
right. She couldn't take care of herself or anyone else either.

When it was time to go she said good-bye
to Mrs. Polarski. "Did I do OK?" she asked,
dreading the answer.

Mrs. Polarski patted her shoulder. "I know
you tried to do your best, but I can only give
you one star today. I'm sure you'll do better
next time."

Emily blinked back tears. Wanda hugged
and kissed her good-bye as though nothing had
happened. Victor and José too. They seemed
to have completely forgotten about the fight
but Emily kept thinking about it as she trudged
back to her homeroom with her single star.

Mr. Davis, her teacher, put it on her chart.
"Only one? That's not like you, Emily. What
happened?"

With her eyes on the floor she told him about the fight.

"Those kids are a handful," he said. "You're doing fine."

"How many stars do I have?"

He counted. "Eighteen."

"How many more do I need for my necklace?"

"Eighty-two."

"Is that a lot?"

"Yes, that's many, many more."

She groaned. "I'll never get all those."

"Sure you will. Don't worry. Now let's get to work." To the whole class he said, "We're going to write a business letter."

Emily sat down at her place beside Donny. Their table had room for two people. A shelf inside held crayons, pencils, and paper. The turkey drawings they had done for Thanksgiving hung on the wall beside the bookcase. But now Mr. Davis handed out paper with lines.

"Write your name, address, and the date in the top right-hand corner of your paper," he said.

Andrea raised her hand. "Teacher, I don't know how."

"Like this." Mr. Davis wrote on the blackboard.

Emily began writing: 580 Fort Washington Avenue. It was hard work to make the letters clear. She licked her lips.

Donny glanced at her paper. "Is that where you live?"

She nodded. "I have my own room."

"I live with my aunt." He showed her his address on his paper. "We have a dog named Brownie. He sleeps on my bed."

"What color eyes does he have?"

"Donny, Emily," Mr. Davis scolded. "Stop talking and get back to work."

After a while he came over to see how they were doing. "Nice, Emily." Mr. Davis smelled good. Emily liked his beard and blue jeans and hiking shoes.

Tom wore blue jeans but her daddy never did. He wore old slacks to work. Once her mother had thrown out a pair of his old pants and he got real mad. He yelled at her. Emily hid in her room till it was all over. Every night when her daddy came home from work he smelled funny and the tips of his fingers were black from stuff he used in his jewelry repair shop. Emily had asked him if she could work in his shop too when she got older. He had laughed and said, "You don't have to worry your pretty little head about working. That's what daddies are for."

But Emily liked getting ink on her fingers, the way she was doing now.

"Big A for Avenue." Mr. Davis wrote over her letter. "See?"

When the two hands of the clock were on the twelve Emily and Donny went to the cafeteria to be helpers.

On the way Emily said, "I'm saving my stars for a perfume-bottle necklace."

"I want the baseball cap," Donny said.

"How many stars do you need?"

"One hundred."

"Me too. How many do you have?"

"Thirty-four."

"Wow." Emily gazed at him in awe.

In the kitchen they signed in and put on aprons and white caps.

Mrs. T., the head cook, tied Emily's apron. "How's my little scooper?"

"I'm going to be an aunt."

Donny looked puzzled. "You're not old enough."

"I am too."

"Sure she is," Mrs. T. said. "Bless your heart, Emily. Is it your sister having a baby? I forget."

"My sister-in-*law*."

"That's right. You told me." Mrs. T. took a baking sheet of grilled cheese sandwiches out of the oven while Emily scooped potato salad into little paper cups. Donny went to the storeroom for plastic trays. He brought them back and counted them.

Emily enjoyed working side-by-side with Mrs. T. She checked her cups and patted her back. "Good work, Emily. No one scoops as nicely as you do. Some of the kids are real sloppy."

Emily blushed. "Thanks." Her spirits soared.

"I don't know what I'll do without you next year." Mrs. T. bustled about getting the sandwiches ready.

"I'll be here," Donny called over his shoulder as he went to the storeroom for more trays.

"No, you won't. You and Emily will be off at high school."

High school. Whenever Emily thought about it she felt scared and excited at the same time. What would it be like? With trembling fingers she set her cups of potato salad on a tray and carefully carried it into the lunchroom.

Around the corner Donny came toward her with a stack of trays piled so high he couldn't see over them.

"Watch out!" Emily shouted.

She stepped out of his way but it was too late. He crashed into her and they both fell down. Trays clattered. Cups flew in all directions. It was just like the time in the supermarket.

Donny landed on top of Emily. He was big and warm. The material of his plaid shirt touched her cheek. She had never been this close to a boy before and could smell his deodorant. Despite herself she smiled.

Mrs. T. let out a shriek. "What's the matter with you two? Look at this mess."

"I'm sorry." Donny disentangled himself from Emily.

Now tears stung her eyes. "It wasn't my fault."

"It wasn't my fault either." They both talked at once.

"OK." Mrs. T. put her hands on her hips. "Tell me what happened. One at a time."

"He bumped into me." Emily scrambled to

her feet and straightened her cap. Bits of potato salad stuck to her apron. Donny reached out and started to brush her off but she pushed his hand away.

"I didn't mean to," he explained. "I couldn't see her."

"Donny, you were carrying too many trays," Mrs. T. said. "Next time don't carry things so high you can't see where you're going. No stars for you today."

"What about me?" Emily asked.

"One star if you help him pick up those trays."

Later, when they were done serving the other kids, they got their own food and went into the lunchroom. Donny sat down next to Emily. She moved away leaving a space between them on the bench. He edged up to her. She leapt up and went to another table. Donny followed her.

"Let's eat together," he said.

"Go away. It's because of you I got into trouble with Mrs. T."

"It was an accident." He perched on the end of her bench.

She let him stay and turned her head away

so that he wouldn't see her smile. Out of the corner of her eye she saw him watching her as she nibbled at her sandwich. Flushed, she remembered falling down with him and wondered if she'd ever be that close to him again.

7

/|||||||\

THE NEXT DAY DONNY BROUGHT EMILY A
present—a package of bubble gum. And the
day after that he brought her a box of Junior
Mints.

"Are you still mad at me?" he asked. They
stood near the washing machine in their classroom.

Emily shrugged, not knowing what to say.

"I'll give you one of my stars," Donny said.
"I'll give you two." He hesitated. "You can
have all of them."

She scratched her elbow. "I want to earn
my own."

Andrea was taking clothes out of the dryer
and overheard them. "Emily has a boyfriend,"
she teased.

"I do not! Mind your own business." Emily

flounced away to her desk and started reading a book about a frog and a toad who were friends. Her cheeks burned.

Donny sat down beside her and read his book too.

Suddenly, sitting next to him sent shivers down her spine.

Another day when they were sorting telephone wires to prepare them for real jobs, Andrea whispered to Emily, "Ricky told me to ask you if you're still mad at Donny."

On the other side of the room Donny seemed to be busy reading a Sears catalogue.

Emily shook her head. "I'm not mad at him."

At recess Andrea whispered something to Ricky who whispered something to Donny and he gave Emily a big smile. When they lined up to go to the computer room Donny asked Emily to be his partner and she said yes. They played Piccadilly together and he matched the most tigers, bees, and spaceships, but she was glad he won.

On the last day of school before Christmas vacation there was a party. The girls brought gifts for the girls and the boys brought gifts for the boys. When it was time to go to their buses Donny took Emily aside and gave her a lumpy package wrapped in green paper printed with red flowers and tied with silver cord.

"It's for you," he said.

"Thanks. What is it?"

"Everybody to the buses," Mr. Davis said, "or they'll leave without you. Have a good holiday! See you next year!"

Emily pulled on her boots and winter coat and hurried to her bus. She waved good-bye to Donny. On the ride home she opened her present. It was a pair of green socks with little Christmas trees embroidered around the cuffs. She wore them all during vacation and showed them to Phyllis at the family Chanukah party.

"Cute." Phyllis leaned closer to get a good look and her big belly got in the way. Emily was surprised that Phyllis was so fat. Every time she saw her she seemed bigger. She sure must be eating an awful lot of candy and Raspberry Newtons. "Where'd you get the socks?"

Emily's cheeks felt hot. "Donny."

Phyllis grinned and tousled Emily's hair. "What a nice present. He must really like you."

"Do you think so?" Emily wanted to talk

about it more but her mother asked her to come into the kitchen and help serve the potato pancakes, and by the time they were finished with dinner, Phyllis said she was fading and wanted to go home to bed.

On the first day back at school Emily wore her Christmas socks. She couldn't wait to show them to Donny, but he was out sick with the flu and didn't return for a long time.

In the middle of January Mr. Davis announced they'd have a special Valentine's Day dance in their room. Would Donny ask her to dance with him? She hoped he wouldn't catch the flu again and be absent.

The week before the party, Emily, Andrea, and Merle made valentine hearts out of red paper and white doilies and hung them up for decorations. The day before the party, Donny, Ricky, and some of the other kids baked cupcakes and frosted them with pink icing and dotted them with candies that said funny things like, "I'm yours," "You're my sweetie," and "Will you be my Valentine?"

When they left for their buses Mr. Davis said, "Don't forget to wear something nice tomorrow."

As soon as Emily got home she called Phyllis and asked her what she should wear.

"What about your red-and-white–checked dress," Phyllis suggested. "The long one."

"It's a baby dress. Cheryl and Amanda never wear dresses like that."

"You look real pretty in it. Red's a good color for you. How about wearing your hair up?"

"I don't know how to do it."

"Maybe I can show you. I wish I could lend you some earrings."

"Daddy won't let me get pierced ears."

"I know . . ." There was a pause, then Phyllis said, "How about wearing something of mine?"

Emily's heart fluttered. "Really? Do you mean it?" It was her dream come true—she was going to wear her big sister's clothes, just like Molly. "What about shoes?"

"What about them?"

"I've only got these dumb saddle shoes."

"Put your mother on. Maybe she'll let me take you shopping for new ones. I need a break from my homework anyway."

That same afternoon Emily and her mother

walked over to Phyllis's. A light snow began to fall. Emily held out her mitten to catch the snowflakes before they melted. The cold air made her breath come out in puffs like smoke as she climbed the hill. Even with her hood on her ears tingled from the cold. But she didn't care and practically ran all the way.

When she and Phyllis were alone in the bedroom, Phyllis took her brush and some pins and arranged Emily's hair on top of her head. Then she opened a drawer in her dresser and pulled out a bright red sweater with long sleeves, red buttons down the front, and shoulder pads. "Would you like to wear this? It'll go with your gray skirt."

Emily gasped. "It's so grown-up! I've never worn anything like that. Mommy makes me wear blouses and dresses to school."

"It's time for a change."

"Are you sure you can lend it?"

Phyllis eyed her big belly. "I won't be wearing it for a while. That's for sure." She helped Emily take off her shirt and put on the sweater.

It was nipped in at the waist and clung tightly. Emily stroked the sleeve. It felt soft and furry like Inky, the pet rabbit at camp.

Then she looked at herself in the mirror and couldn't believe what she saw. The girl reflected there didn't look like the old Emily at all. She looked like Phyllis and Cheryl and Amanda. What would Donny say when he saw her?

Emily threw her arms around Phyllis's neck and hugged her so tight she yelled, "Stop! I can't breathe." Emily's hair tumbled down and they both laughed.

Suddenly Phyllis put her hand on her belly. "The baby's kicking. Want to feel it?"

Emily nodded. Phyllis took her hand and pressed it gently where Phyllis's had been. At first Emily didn't feel anything. Then something pushed against her hand. Then again, harder.

Emily grinned. "The baby."

Phyllis's eyes were shining. "That's some strong kid in there. When Tom comes home at night and talks to the baby it leans toward him."

"It does?" Something bothered Emily. "Phyllis, how will it get out?"

Phyllis hesitated. Emily knew she had said something wrong and her elbow started to itch. But Phyllis went to her nightstand and pulled out a book. She showed Emily a picture of a mommy with a baby upside down in her tummy. The next picture showed the baby sliding out. Emily stared and stared.

Then she giggled. "I used to think a baby came out of your mouth."

Phyllis said, "Now you know." She checked her watch. "It's getting late. We'd better go. I'll help you change back into your blouse."

On the way to the store Emily kept glancing sideways at Phyllis and squeezing her hand. When they passed the Stork Baby Shop Phyllis stopped to look at the window display.

"We'll have to go shopping for baby clothes soon," she murmured. "I like that natural pine crib over there with polka-dot sheets and dust ruffle. What do you think?"

Emily said nothing. She wasn't looking at the cribs. Her eyes focused on their reflection in the window. Phyllis was so big her coat didn't button. Emily looked puny beside her.

"I wonder how much that crib costs," Phyllis said and led the way into the store.

Hannah waved to Emily. She was busy with a bunch of customers and called, "I'll be with you in a few minutes. Look around."

Phyllis wandered over to the pine crib and

Emily followed. She stared at the empty crib where the baby would sleep.

"Phyllis," she began, "there's something I want to ask you, but promise you won't get mad."

"What is it?"

"Promise."

"Shoot."

In a low voice Emily said, "Do you really have to take your top off in front of a boy to have a baby?"

Phyllis smiled. "It's not that you *have* to, but you *want* to. Remember I told you about the kissing and loving and getting very close?"

Emily nodded, her eyes on the crib mattress. "And do you have to do all those other things too?"

"When you're grown-up and married there's a right time for it."

"But I can't tell time," Emily said.

"This is a different kind of time." Phyllis examined a price tag dangling from one of the bars of the crib. She pulled off her gloves and ran her hand along the top rail. "Sometimes the mother and father do those things even when they don't want to have a child."

Emily shifted uncomfortably from one foot to the other. "Why? What do you mean?"

"When people love each other like Tom and me, and your mother and father, they want to do those things and be very close."

"Yuck!" Emily made a face.

"It won't seem yucky when you're older. You'll understand it then."

Emily gazed longingly at a lamp shaped like a duck, sitting on a dresser. The lamp had a plaid lampshade and gave a warm, glowy light.

"I get my period," she whispered confidentially. "I used to think that meant I could have babies but Molly said that was dumb."

"No, that's not dumb," Phyllis said. "That means your body's getting ready."

"That's what Mommy said."

"But it doesn't mean you're completely ready yet. The thing is, Emily, that people don't have babies themselves or with angels. The man and the woman make the baby together."

"Can we buy that duck lamp for the baby?" Emily asked.

Just then the other customers left the shop and Hannah came over to them.

"This is my sister-in-law, Phyllis," Emily said.

"Emily's going to be a wonderful help to you," Hannah said. She showed Phyllis how the crib could change into a bed when the baby got older, and Phyllis said she would come back and look at it again with Tom.

From the Stork Baby Shop she and Emily hurried to Joseph's Shoe Store before it closed. The sky was turning deep blue and the street-lights had already come on. Inside the shoe store Phyllis asked, "Do you know what you want?"

Emily spotted lace-up boots with little heels and pointy toes and showed them to the shoe man. After he measured her foot Phyllis told him to bring a pair in her size.

"Black or brown?" he asked.

"Black," Emily said and Phyllis nodded in agreement.

Emily sat on the edge of her seat and waited in suspense. What if he didn't have a pair in her size? What if they cost too much money?

After what seemed like hours the shoe man returned with a box. "The last one in black. These have been our best seller." He slipped the boots on Emily's feet and tied the long laces.

She walked to the mirror without wobbling and stole a look at herself. She was so excited she forgot all about babies and duck lamps. In these shoes she looked like a different person—tall, graceful, a regular teenage girl.

"They look great," Phyllis said. "Like them?"

"I love them!" Emily ran over to Phyllis and kissed her.

"Easy!" Phyllis laughed. "Let's get a pair of tights for you too. Want to wear the shoes home?"

"Oh, no. I'll save them for tomorrow." Emily pictured how she would look on Valentine's Day. It was going to be the best day of her life. She knew it.

8

⁂

THE NEXT MORNING EMILY PUT ON THE RED
sweater and her new shoes. She went into the
kitchen for breakfast. Her father was making
coffee. She stood there waiting for him to tell
her how pretty she looked.

"What have you got on?" he said.

"Phyllis's red sweater. She lent it to me."

He eyed her lace-up boots with the little
heels and pointy toes. "And where did you get
those?"

"At the store, yesterday. Phyllis took me.
Mommy said it was OK." Emily held out her
foot. "Aren't they beautiful?"

"You're not going to school dressed like that,
are you?"

Emily scratched her elbow. She went to the
cupboard to get a bowl for her Froot Loops.
"We're having a dance for Valentine's Day."

"I don't want you wearing that sweater."
Her father brought his coffee to the small table
and sat down.

"Why not?" Emily leaned against the wall.

"It's too old for you."

"What do you mean?"

"It makes you look older than you are. This
is not my little Emily."

"You don't like me anymore since I've gotten big."

"That's not true. You're my precious baby."

"Don't call me baby anymore!" Emily
shouted. "Don't ever call me baby again!"

Her mother hurried into the kitchen. She
was still wearing her bathrobe. "What are you
two arguing about?"

"Daddy won't let me wear this sweater to
school."

Emily's mother looked her over. "Maybe
Daddy's right, honey. It's a little . . . grown-
up."

"I want to be grown-up. Phyllis said it
looked good on me."

"I'm sure Phyllis meant well," her mother
said, "but we're your parents and we know
what's best for you."

"Phyllis said it was time for a change."

Emily's father banged down his coffee mug. "Phyllis, Phyllis. All I hear is Phyllis."

"She's my sister-in-law!"

"Emily," her mother said firmly, "your bus will be here in a few minutes. Now go to your room and put on another top. How about your pink blouse with the lace collar?"

"That's a baby blouse," Emily said.

"Do as I say and make it snappy."

Emily stormed out of the kitchen. She heard her father say to her mother, "What's the matter with her?"

"Hush," her mother said. "She's growing up."

In her room Emily pulled the red sweater over her head, folded it and stuffed it into her backpack. Then she yanked her dumb blouse off the hanger and put it on. She trudged into the hallway and pulled on her winter coat.

"There," her mother said sweetly. "You look pretty as a picture. What a good girl."

With a pang Emily thought about the sweater hidden in her backpack. She looked away when her mother kissed her good-bye.

"I'll walk you down to the bus," her father said.

"No. I want to go myself." Emily marched out of the apartment and took the elevator down to the lobby.

All the way to school on the bus the pack felt heavy and hot. When she got to school Emily dashed into the girls' bathroom. Quickly she changed out of her blouse and into the red sweater. When she went into her classroom Emily felt everyone looking at her. She smiled.

Later, in the cafeteria, Mrs. T. pulled Emily's apron up high and tied it tightly under her arms to protect her sweater, and warned her not to get food spattered on her new shoes.

"Don't you look smart!" she said.

Donny had said nothing in the classroom but Emily could tell he noticed that today she looked different. Now he said, "Red's pretty. Red is for Valentine's Day."

After lunch Mr. Davis helped them set up the refreshments and push back the tables and chairs to clear a space. "Dance time," he said.

Andrea had brought a mixed hip-hop tape and put it in the cassette player. She and Merle got up and danced first, then the others joined in, one by one. Donny didn't move. Emily sat in her seat wondering why he didn't ask her to dance. The beat of the music stirred her. She rocked from side to side and tapped her feet. Finally Ricky asked her to dance, then Leon. She shot Donny a look signaling him to cut in but he didn't budge.

"Get in there and dance," Mr. Davis urged him.

Donny shook his head.

"Come on, it's easy." Mr. Davis did a few steps of the Electric Slide.

Emily and Andrea giggled. "Teacher's dancing."

Donny sat there by himself, watching.

Gathering up her courage, Emily went over to him. "Come on, Donny. Dance with us." She took his hand and led him to the floor.

"I don't know how," he mumbled.

"My brother taught me." She stepped in, slid her foot along till it was touching the other, then did a little stomp. She moved in time to the music the way Tom had shown her, the way they did on TV.

The singers on the tape sang loud and fast. *Boom chick-chick boom.* She bounced her head back and forth and sometimes snapped her fingers. She had just learned to do that. Donny snapped his fingers too. Awkwardly he moved his shoulder and shuffled his feet a little, imitating her.

"That's right!" she exclaimed. "You're getting it."

A slower song came on and people paired off. Emily left her arms outstretched. Donny took her hands and they swayed in time to the music. His hands were warm but not sweaty. He held hers just right—firmly and not too tight. As they danced she looked into his eyes. He looked back into hers and smiled a little. It felt as though no one else was in the room except them.

Emily wanted the song to go on forever. The next one was faster. They separated and, facing each other, danced more hip-hop, but Emily still felt happy. When the bell rang it was time to push the tables back into place and go home. Emily was hot and out of breath, as if she had been jumping rope. She left her coat unbuttoned.

At the buses Donny reached into his backpack and handed her an envelope. She tore it open. Inside was a valentine showing two teddy bears. It was signed, "To Emily from Donny."

"Thanks." She tucked it into her backpack.

On the way home she kept thinking about dancing with Donny. She could still hear the music in her head.

When she got off the bus she saw Patrick Duggan. He was standing outside her building and smoking a cigarette. He seemed to be alone. Even though it was freezing he wasn't wearing gloves or a hat, and the tips of his ears were red. Overhead the sky was dark. It looked as though a snowstorm was coming.

"What are you all dressed up for?" he asked.

"We had a Valentine's Day party at school."

Patrick stared at her in an odd kind of way. He flicked his cigarette butt into the street. "What do they do at that school of yours?"

"Oh, dance."

Patrick looked surprised. "Dance?"

"Today we did the Electric Slide."

"You're cuter than you used to be."

The way he looked at her made her feel funny. She reached under her hood and pushed a piece of hair behind her ear.

"I like that sweater," he said.

She pulled her coat around her and suddenly remembered she wasn't supposed to be wearing the sweater. Her heart started beating fast.

"My sister-in-law let me borrow it for the party."

Patrick hunched his shoulders. He wore a bulky denim jacket with a white furry collar. The collar was turned up. A package of cigarettes poked out of a pocket. He looked around and so did Emily, but they were the only people on the street. He rubbed his hands together and blew into them. "Did your brother get married?"

"Yes, to Phyllis. They're going to have a baby."

Patrick looked at her legs and lace-up boots. Then he pointed to some letters written in chalk on the sidewalk. "Do you know what that means?"

Emily shook her head. She had seen those letters lots of times but her mother said not to say it because it was a bad word.

Patrick took her hand and through her mitten made circles in her palm with his finger. "Do you know what that means?" His voice was very low.

"It tickles." She giggled.

He didn't smile. "What are you doing now?"

"I have to go home. I'm supposed to go

straight home when I get off the bus. My mommy waits for me." Emily wondered how she'd slip into the apartment without her mother seeing her in the red sweater.

"What time do you usually get home?"

"Mommy says three-thirty."

Patrick pushed back his sleeve and looked at his watch. "Your bus must have been early today. It's only ten after three." He showed Emily his watch. It had no numbers at all, only the face of a cartoon cat with a big white eye winking at her. Patrick put his finger in his mouth and chewed his nail.

"Good-bye." Emily started walking toward the entrance of her building.

"Hey, wait a minute! I have a new Diamond Back. Want to see it?"

She stopped and turned around. "What's that?"

"The hottest dirt bike on the market."

Sometimes Patrick was mean, but today he was being very nice. Once when she was little he took her new rubber ball away and wouldn't give it back. When she came home crying and told Tom, he went to Patrick's building with her and made him return it.

"I'll let you sit on the bike," Patrick said now. "Come on—just for a minute."

Emily had never been on a Diamond Back. She didn't even know how to ride a two-wheeler yet. Her father said bikes were too dangerous to ride in the city, although he had let Tom have one when he was a teenager. Tom had kept it parked in the front hall and had given her lessons sometimes. Emily remembered.

"You can even squeeze the hand brakes," Patrick was saying.

"Okay." Emily followed Patrick down the street to his building.

Inside it was hot. She pulled off her mittens and stuffed them into her pockets. They went up some steps into the lobby, then past a mail room, and down a flight of stairs to the laundry room.

"In here," Patrick said.

It was dark. Emily smelled soap powder and heard clothes spinning in one of the dryers. All of a sudden she felt she shouldn't be there. Patrick pulled a string hanging from the ceiling and turned on a light. It was still kind of gloomy.

"This way," he said.

Beyond the washers and dryers there was a door. It was closed. A padlock hung from the latch. Patrick held the padlock toward the light and, peering closely at it, twirled the dial. He unfastened the lock and opened the door.

"My bike's in the storeroom," he said. "Come on."

"I don't want to go in there."

"Come on," he coaxed.

Emily shook her head. "It's too dark."

"OK. Wait here." He went into the storeroom and brought out his bike.

"Oh," Emily gasped. It was black and very shiny with lots of silver trim.

He put down the kickstand. "Want to try it?"

"I don't know how."

"Just sit on it. It will be easier without your coat."

She slipped it off along with her backpack and he helped her on, keeping one hand on her waist.

"I'm falling!" She grabbed the handlebars.

"Don't worry," Patrick said. "I've got you."

He was standing so close to her she could

hear him breathing. He was breathing hard. She wanted to push him away but was afraid to let go of the handlebars. He put his face near hers. His hair was against her cheek. Then he tightened his grip on her waist and kissed her on the lips. He tasted awful, like cigarette smoke. His face covered hers. She couldn't breathe.

When you want a baby you kiss very long and get the closest you can get. What was Patrick doing?

Furious, Emily let go of the handlebars and socked him on the shoulder. They both came crashing down with the bike on her leg. The wheels spun and the spokes rattled.

"You little dummy!" Patrick pinned her down.

Emily struggled to get free but he was too big. His weight was crushing her. She pushed at him with all her might. He didn't budge. She kicked him with her pointy-toed boot. He held fast and brought his lips towards hers. Quickly she turned her face away so that he couldn't kiss her again. This wasn't at all like the time Donny fell down with her. It wasn't like being close to Donny when they danced.

"Let me go!" she yelled and burst into tears. "You're hurting me!"

"What the heck are you kids doing over there?" Someone carrying a basket of clothes came into the laundry room. "I'm calling the super!"

Patrick jumped up and picked up his bike. "*Crybaby! Dummy!* You'd better not tell your mother!"

Her new tights were ripped. Underneath her leg was bleeding. Emily scrambled to her feet, grabbed her coat and backpack, squeezed past the woman holding the laundry basket, and ran.

9

EMILY RAN INTO HER APARTMENT, SOBBING. SHE clutched at her coat and wrapped it high around her neck. Her hands were shaking.

"Emily! Don't you even say hello?" Her mother tried to stop her but Emily pulled away and ran past her into her bedroom. She slammed the door shut.

"Where have you been?" her mother called. "It's late! What happened at the party?"

The party seemed far away. Emily could never tell her mother what had happened. She knew she had done something bad. It was her fault. She shouldn't have gone into the laundry room with Patrick. She shouldn't have worn the red sweater. She shouldn't have sneaked it out of the house. Carelessly she pulled it off, threw it under her bed, grabbed the stupid pink blouse from the backpack, and hurriedly put it on. If only she had worn it in the first place.

She went into the bathroom and washed her face to get rid of Patrick's kiss, Patrick's smell.

When she came out her mother said, "Emily, tell me what happened." She held her at arm's length and looked her over from head to torn tights. "My goodness, you did your buttons up wrong." She seemed concerned. Then she undid Emily's buttons and fastened them up the right way. "Did somebody hurt you? Did you get into a fight?"

"I fell down and tore my tights."

Her mother rocked her in her arms and stroked her hair. "My poor baby. Mommy will get you a Band-Aid."

From her mother's room came Phyllis's voice. "Emily, how was the party? Come here and tell me."

What was she doing there? Emily wondered. She dried her eyes and went in. Phyllis was lying on the big bed, her glasses off. Emily wanted to tell her about Patrick. She would understand and make the bad feeling go away. Emily sat down next to her and took her hand.

"Guess what?" Phyllis said in a tired voice. "I'm having pains."

Emily frowned. "What kind of pains?"

"The baby might be coming but it's way too early. It's not ready to be born yet. Your mother took me to see the doctor and he wants me to stay off my feet and rest."

"Phyllis, I have to tell you something."

"I'm so worried." Phyllis started to cry. Tears trickled down her cheeks and onto the pillow.

Emily had never seen her cry before and didn't know what to do.

Phyllis wiped her eyes with the back of her hand and sniffled. "I don't want anything to happen to the baby."

Emily's mother bustled into the room. "Now stop that. Nothing's going to happen to that baby. You're going to do just fine. How about a cup of tea? Emily, come into the kitchen and help me."

While Emily put cookies on a plate, her mother said, "Tell me how your tights got ripped. Did you trip on the bus?"

Emily said nothing.

Her mother poured boiling water into the

flowered teapot. "Of all the days for you to be late . . . That's just what I needed—"

"You never listen to me!" Emily blurted out.

"Of course I listen to you. I'm listening to you now." Her mother took mugs out of the cupboard.

"You didn't ask about the party."

Her mother arranged the teapot and mugs on a tray and said, "Look, Emily, Phyllis has labor pains. This is serious. Sometimes other people need me more. You have to understand."

Emily started to cry and all the bad things that had happened in the basement filled her mind.

Her mother patted her back. "You're just tired. You've had a big day. Why don't you take a cookie to your room and lie down?"

Emily snatched a cookie and stomped off to her room. Nobody thought about anything but Phyllis and her baby.

For the next few weeks Phyllis had to stay home in her bed. She couldn't even come out to the park to watch the St. Patrick's Day parade go by. One day, when it was warm enough for Emily to wear her jacket instead of her winter coat, her mother dropped her off at Phyllis's to help tidy up the kitchen and keep her company. First they looked at a catalogue of hiking and biking clothes.

Emily said, "Phyllis, something happened."

"H'm?" She turned a page.

"Patrick did something bad to me."

Phyllis put down the catalogue and looked hard at Emily. "What did he do?"

"He kissed me when I was wearing your red sweater, the one you lent me. Daddy didn't want me to wear it, but I wanted to be more grown-up like you. I sneaked it out of the house and wore it anyway." Emily watched Phyllis closely to see what she would say or do.

Phyllis said, "I used to do things like that too. Tell me more about Patrick."

"He's a boy on my street. He smoked a cigarette and the bike fell on us."

"Is that all?"

Emily nodded.

Phyllis rolled over on her side. "Listen. Some boys can be rotten."

"Which boys?"

"OK, how did you happen to be alone with him in the first place?"

"He told me he had a new bike and we went to see it."

"Where?"

"In his building, in the basement."

Phyllis sighed. "Oh, Emily. Why did you go with him?"

"I wanted to see his bike. He let me sit on it."

"Emily, there are nice boys and not-so-nice boys. You've got to learn the difference. Did you really think he wanted to show you his bike?"

Emily did, but she knew that was the wrong answer.

"Sometimes boys want to get you alone in a room," Phyllis said. "They want to kiss you and touch you, but you can't let them."

"Why?"

"You have to know which boys you can trust."

"*How* do you know?"

"Remember what we said about loving and being close? Sometimes it's fine to touch and kiss, like when you love someone and know them very well, like Tom and me."

Emily twirled a strand of hair around her finger. "I've known Patrick for a long time."

"But is he really your friend?"

Emily shook her head and said, "No." It was so confusing. "A lady came down and yelled at us, Phyllis."

"Oh, Lord, Emily. Thank goodness." She threw up her hands. "I don't know how I can explain any better."

"Everyone says I have to know things," Emily shouted, "and nobody helps me! I thought you'd help me."

"I'm trying," she said.

"You don't care. All you care about is that baby." Emily glared at Phyllis's big belly.

Phyllis didn't say anything for a moment. Then she reached *way* over and held out her arms to Emily. She gave her a little kiss. "Emily, honey, I know it's hard to figure out, but you'll get it."

In the kitchen she felt more alone than when she was really alone, like when her mother went shopping and her daddy was at work. And there were so many dirty dishes piled up in the sink she didn't know where to start.

She turned on the hot water and a few drops trickled out. All of a sudden there was a loud banging and the water shot out of the faucet and splashed the front of her blouse. She was so surprised she jumped away. Then she grabbed the dish towel and tried to dry her blouse but the wet spots stuck to her. The water was pouring out of the faucet and filling up the sink.

Emily wished her mother would come and get her. Tears stung her eyes as she went back to the sink and turned down the water so the right amount came out. At home when she did the dishes her mother would tell her if it was her turn to wash or dry. While they worked they'd talk about new clothes or what they'd have for dinner the next day, and when all the dishes were done and put away her mother would thank her for helping and say, "Emily, you're good as gold."

Now Emily took the top dish and soaped it with the sponge. A piece of food was stuck to the dark blue picture of a tree. She scrubbed and scrubbed but it wouldn't come off. Tears ran down her cheeks. Couldn't Phyllis hear her crying?

She stopped to wipe her nose and knocked over a can of cleanser with her elbow. Green powder sprinkled the floor. Emily howled but Phyllis didn't come.

The next morning Emily's mother woke her up early even though it was Saturday. "Phyllis had the baby!" she shouted. "A little girl. She was born at three-thirty this morning."

Emily felt goose bumps. "A baby girl! I want to see her."

"You will. We'll go right after breakfast."

In the kitchen her daddy was making coffee. He beamed. "Now Phyllis is a mother, Tom is a father, we're grandparents, and Emily, you're an aunt." He poured coffee and sat down at the table. "A new baby changes every-one's life."

Emily certainly hoped so. Perhaps now Phyllis would be her regular self again and they'd talk and do things together.

On the way to the hospital they stopped at the florist's and got Phyllis a big bunch of pink spring flowers—tulips, roses, and sweet peas.

"But her favorite color is blue," Emily said.

"Pink is for the baby," her mother told her.

In the hospital gift shop Emily bought her own gift for Phyllis—a box of Mason's Dots, their favorite candy. They took an elevator up to the second floor and a nurse at the desk directed them to Phyllis's room. Walking down the hall Emily wondered if Phyllis would look different now.

Phyllis was lying in bed wearing a little jacket over her nightgown and a blue ribbon tied around her hair. Tom was sitting in a chair beside her. He looked tired and needed a shave. Emily ran over to him and hugged him. His stubble scratched her face. Then she threw her arms around Phyllis and hugged and kissed her.

"Careful," Phyllis laughed. "You're steaming up my glasses."

Emily giggled and gave her the Dots. Her mother hugged Phyllis and gave her the flowers.

Phyllis smelled them. "They're gorgeous, Isabelle. Thanks." She made room for them next to a vase shaped like a baby shoe, filled with pink carnations. Emily noticed the open box of chocolates sitting on a stack of fashion magazines. Just as she had thought. Having a baby must be fun.

Her father clapped Tom on the back and

kissed him. Then he gave Phyllis a kiss on the cheek. "So where's my granddaughter? When do I get to see her?"

Tom grinned. "We'll go down to the nursery in a few minutes."

"Is she . . . okay?" Emily's mother faltered. "Does she have all her fingers and toes?"

"The pediatrician saw her early this morning," Phyllis answered, "and said she seems fine."

"How are you feeling, dear? Did you have a hard time?"

"It hurt but Tom was right there, and guess what I did after?"

"What?" Emily leaned closer.

"I ate a piece of cherry pie."

Tom took her hand. "She was great. A real trooper."

Emily's father picked up a rubber tube from a chair. It was like the kind the little kids at camp used for swimming. "Is it all right if I sit here?"

"Sure," Phyllis said.

Emily wondered if she went swimming in the hospital. "What's the tube for?"

"To sit on so my stitches won't hurt."

"What stitches?" One summer at camp Molly fell and cut her chin. She had to have five stitches and wear a bandage, but Emily didn't see any bandage on Phyllis.

Phyllis rolled her eyes.

"I'll explain to you later," Emily's mother said.

Later, later. Always later. Emily knew she had said something wrong and her elbow started to itch. When would she get things right? When would she be alone with Phyllis and have another chance to really talk to her?

Tom stood up and put his arm around his mother's shoulders. "Come on, I'll take you to see your granddaughter."

"Have you decided on a name?"

Tom and Phyllis looked at each other and smiled.

"Jessica," she said. "It was a compromise."

"I like that name," Emily said.

Phyllis got out of bed and put on her slippers. She leaned on Tom's arm as they walked to the nursery. Emily pressed her face to the window and nearly swooned when she saw all the babies swaddled in their blankets, nestled in their plastic bassinets. Some of them were sleeping, some were crying, a couple wore knitted hats. They looked so cuddly she wanted to pick them all up and hold them in her arms.

"Which one is ours?" her father asked.

"Over there." Tom pointed to a baby in the second row. A card with a pink border was taped to the head of her bassinet. "Isn't she beautiful?"

Emily thrilled at her first glimpse of Jessica. Her face was kind of red and she had lots of dark hair. Clearly she was the best baby in the nursery. Emily loved her right away.

"Oh, Tom," her mother said in a voice that sounded like crying. "She's lovely."

Emily's father said nothing but there was a big smile on his face and his eyes looked wet.

Emily wanted to stay and look at Jessica forever, but Phyllis said, "Let's go back to the room. They'll be bringing the babies in soon for feeding."

Before they left Phyllis showed them a picture of Jessica that was taken right after she was born and gave one to Emily. Clutching her picture Emily stopped at the nursery one more time to see her niece and blew her a kiss through the window.

"Someday *I'll* have a baby in the nursery,"

she said. For the moment she put out of her mind the things Phyllis and her mother had told her.

"Isabelle," her father said sharply, "I thought we settled this."

"Oh, Irv," her mother said. "Emily doesn't mean anything by it. Do you, dear?"

10

∧∥∥∥∥∧

AT SCHOOL ON MONDAY EMILY SHOWED THE picture to everyone. "Mr. Davis, I'm an aunt. This is Jessica."

He looked at the photo. "Nice baby, Emily. Congratulations."

"But I haven't held her yet."

"I'm sure you will."

What if I don't? Maybe Tom and Phyllis won't let me. Maybe they think I don't know how because my head doesn't work right, she thought. If I could just hold the baby I'd be different.

When she showed the picture to Donny he grinned. "I like babies. What's her name?"

"Jessica."

"There's a little boy who lives next door to me. I play with him and sometimes I watch him while his mother goes to the store."

"Do you think I'll be able to watch Jessica and take care of her?"

Donny looked into her eyes. "I'd let you, Emily."

Side by side they made drawings for the baby. Emily did a purple house, flowers, a tree, and a sun wearing glasses. Donny drew his dog, Brownie. Sometimes Donny's shoulder brushed hers. Sometimes their fingers touched when they reached for crayons at the same time, and Emily tingled.

When she got home she showed the drawings to her mother.

"Very nice, dear. You can take them to Jessica tonight. She's home from the hospital."

"Will I get to hold her?"

"Maybe. There's no time to talk about it now, dear. I'm in a rush." Emily's mother busily cooked chicken and wrapped some in aluminum foil for Tom and Phyllis.

After dinner Emily's father drove them to Tom and Phyllis's in his car. As soon as Emily walked into the apartment she noticed a different smell, like Johnson's Baby Powder. Although it wasn't bedtime yet Phyllis was wearing her blue quilted bathrobe. She looked very tired.

Emily gave her the drawings. "They're for Jessica. Donny did this one." She held out the portrait of Brownie.

Phyllis said, "Thanks, honey," but she hardly looked at them.

Tom took them into the bedroom. The only light came from a shaded lamp on the dresser. He taped the pictures up on the wall near Jessica's pine crib with polka-dot sheets and dust ruffle. "Look what Aunt Em and her friend made for you," he whispered.

In the shadows Emily stood there watching the baby sleep. She was so tiny she hardly took up any space at all. She lay on her side propped against a rolled-up blanket. Another blanket printed with ducks covered her. Only her face peeped out.

"I want to hold her," Emily said.

Tom shook his head. "Not till she wakes up."

"Why?"

"We have to let her sleep."

"I want to hold her *now*." Emily's voice rose.

"Shh. You'll wake her."

"You don't want me to hold her!"

"Honey, that's not true."

"You think I don't know how. If she were

my baby I could pick her up whenever I liked."

"Emily, what's gotten into you? This is no time for a tantrum. Behave yourself." He grasped her arm but she jerked away and stomped off to the living room.

Phyllis was sitting on her tube in the rocking chair.

Emily's father gave her a slim box. "This is for the baby."

Phyllis opened it and gasped. "Oh, Irv." She held up a tiny gold bracelet.

Emily went over to see it. "What does it say?" She pointed to the letters.

"That's Jessica's name." Phyllis spelled it for her.

"Daddy, will you get one for my baby?" Emily blurted out. "Her name will be Janet."

There was a hush.

"What's she talking about?" her father said to her mother.

"I can have babies if I want to," Emily explained. "I know all about it. Phyllis showed me a book."

"For crying out loud, do we have to go through that again?"

"It's all right, Irv." Emily's mother patted

his arm and started chattering about Jessica's resemblance to Tom.

A week later when Emily went to see the baby she promised herself she wouldn't leave till she got to hold her even if she had to stay all night. She brought Jessica a present she had bought with her own money. It was a rattle shaped like a rose. Her mother's best friend, Bea, came along for the visit carrying a white box tied with pink ribbons.

"What's in the box?" Emily asked at the front door.

"Something for the baby."

Through the door Emily could hear Jessica crying. Good, she said to herself. This time she's awake.

Emily's mother rang the buzzer.

"Just a minute!" Phyllis called.

"Does she know I'm coming?" Bea whispered.

"Don't worry," Emily's mother said. "She loves company."

The door opened. Phyllis was wearing one of Tom's old shirts and a pair of his old army shorts. Her hair was uncombed and she was barefoot. Emily had never seen her look like that before.

When she saw Bea she scowled. "I wasn't expecting company."

Bea smiled anyway and gave her the box. "I just wanted to bring this to the baby. I'll only stay a few minutes."

Emily gave Phyllis the rattle and she let them into the apartment.

It was a mess. A rack of drying baby clothes stood in the middle of the living room. The carriage was parked next to the couch. The breakfast dishes were still on the table along with gift baskets of flowers and balloons. Emily's wedding present plant looked like it hadn't been watered in a long time. She poked the soil with her finger. Sure enough, it was dry.

"Did you get any sleep, dear?" Emily's mother asked Phyllis.

"I'm exhausted," she mumbled. "The baby was up all night."

Just then Jessica started to cry.

"I'll get her," Emily offered.

"Let me," her mother said.

"I will." Phyllis stumbled toward the bedroom.

While she was gone Emily's mother gave Bea a look. "As soon as we see the baby, we'll go."

Bea nodded in agreement.

When Phyllis came back into the room carrying the baby they gathered around her, clucking and offering praises.

Jessica whimpered.

"She probably wants to eat again," Phyllis said.

"How do you know?" Emily asked.

"When she cries I figure it can only be a couple of things—either she needs to be fed, changed, or held."

Emily touched the baby's tiny hand. Jessica grasped Emily's finger and stopped crying. "She likes me!"

"Of course." Her mother took the baby in her arms. "You're her auntie."

"Can I hold her?"

Phyllis lowered herself into the rocking chair and arranged a pillow under her arm. "After I feed her. She's kind of fussy now."

Emily's mother handed the baby back to Phyllis.

"You let everybody hold her but me," Emily grumbled.

"Be patient." Her mother shot her a warning look.

Emily stood there fuming. When Phyllis asked her to open the white box for her, she yanked off the ribbon and ripped the tissue paper. Inside were a sunsuit and matching bonnet.

"Thanks, Bea." Phyllis smiled. "What a cute outfit."

"I got the six-month size," Bea said. "I wasn't sure what size to get. The saleslady said small but I thought the baby might be too big for it by summer—"

"It's adorable," Emily's mother interrupted. "Come on. We don't want to overstay our welcome."

"Do we have to go?" Emily wailed. "I didn't get to hold the baby. Not once."

"It's up to Phyllis." Her mother hesitated. "I'd like to stay and help if she'd let me."

"I don't need any help," Phyllis said sharply.

"How about if Emily stays here for a while and does some dishes? I could come back and get her later and bring you and Tom something from the delicatessen for dinner."

"Please, could I?" Emily clasped her hands and hopped up and down in anticipation.

"Fine," Phyllis said crisply over the baby's cries.

When her mother and Bea had left, Emily began by filling a glass with cold water and bringing it into the living room.

"Where are you going with that glass?" Phyllis snapped.

She had never talked to Emily in that tone of voice before.

"I'm watering the plant I gave you."

"Thanks. At least *you* remembered. And don't look at me that way. You can't expect me to water plants when I have all this to do." Phyllis waved her arm towards the drying baby clothes.

Tears came to Emily's eyes. She felt cold inside as though it were snowing. At home she had a glass toy with a snowman. When she shook it up snowflakes fell silently. That's how she felt now. Cold and quiet. Her eyes brimmed with tears as she emptied her glass of water into the pot and trudged back to the kitchen. All she was good for was washing dishes, she told herself. And she couldn't even do that very well on her own. The last time at Phyllis's she had made a big mess and had gotten all wet.

Now, at the sink, she turned on the water, dug out a sponge, squirted liquid soap on it, and took the top dish. The rest of the stack toppled with a terrible clatter.

Emily screeched and jumped back, panic-stricken. Not again! Had she broken any dishes?

"Emily," Phyllis shouted, "what happened?"

"Nothing."

Water dripped on the floor from the dish and sponge she was holding. She couldn't do anything right, not even dishwashing. No wonder Phyllis wouldn't let her hold Jessica.

"Leave the dishes," Phyllis said. "I'm going to feed the baby. Come in here with me."

Emily put down her dish and sponge and turned off the water. In the living room she shoved aside a large package of disposable diapers and sat down on the couch. To her utter amazement Phyllis pulled open the top button of her shirt, unsnapped a flap on her bra and drew it down.

"What are you doing?" Emily asked, averting her eyes.

"I'm nursing the baby. I have milk for her."

"Do you do that when Tom is here?"

"Sure."

Curiosity forced Emily to steal a glance at Phyllis from the corner of her eye. She was pushing the baby up to get her started.

Emily sat there transfixed. It was hard to believe milk came from Phyllis's body. It was weird and nice at the same time. Phyllis didn't seem to mind. Her eyes were fastened on the baby. The only sound was Jessica sucking. A peaceful quiet filled the room.

After a while Phyllis put the baby over her shoulder and gently patted her back. Jessica burped. Emily giggled. It was funny to hear such a loud noise coming from such a little baby. At school when Ricky burped it was gross. Sometimes Emily thought he did it on purpose.

Phyllis switched the baby to her other side and rocked while she nursed her. The creak of her rocking chair lulled Emily. She settled back against the cushions and watched every move so that she'd know what to do when she had a baby of her own. Of course, there was the awful part, but she didn't want to think about that now. Not with Jessica here. And if she didn't practice with Jessica she'd never learn.

All of a sudden Phyllis said, "Would you like to hold her now?"

Emily sat up straight. She was so excited she was nearly scared. What if she didn't do it right? What if she dropped the baby? Could she be trusted?

"First, wash your hands," Phyllis said.

Emily ran to the bathroom, scrubbed, and hurried back.

"Sit way back on the couch," Phyllis said, "and make a cradle with your arms. Hold the baby's head up."

Emily bent her arms and held them stiffly outstretched. Phyllis placed the baby there, making sure her head was supported.

A shiver ran down Emily's spine. With Jessica in her arms she felt like a real mother. She wished Donny could see her. The warmth of

Jessica reminded her of him. She remembered how good he felt when she fell down with him in the cafeteria, and the way their fingers touched when they were drawing and dancing. She smiled and softly started singing.

11

/|\||

NOT LONG AFTERWARD EMILY WAS WATCHING TV one evening while her mother read the newspaper.

"Emily," her mother said, "it will be your birthday in a couple of weeks. Daddy and I want to take you to see this show." She held up the newspaper and pointed to an ad.

"What show?"

"It's called *Annie*, with real live actors and actresses singing and dancing on a stage. Would you like to invite a friend?"

"Donny!" Emily shouted.

Her mother put down the paper on the couch. "Isn't there some girl you'd like to ask?"

"You said a friend. Donny's my friend."

Her mother looked thoughtful. "What

about one of the girls in your class?"

"I like Donny. A lot of girls in my class like boys and Mr. Davis says that's OK. We dance together and have parties."

"Look, Emily." Her mother breathed hard. "That isn't what your father and I had in mind. I asked you to invite a girlfriend."

"You don't want me to have fun." Emily switched off the TV. "I want to see Donny on my birthday."

"Oh, my goodness, Emily, what's gotten into you? Why are you being so difficult?"

"You're just scared of what Daddy will say. He never wants me to have any fun!"

"Emily Ann Gold! Go to your room this minute!"

"I'll be glad to!" Emily stormed off to her bedroom and slammed the door shut.

Later, when she was in bed, her mother came in to kiss her good-night. Emily turned away and faced the wall.

Her mother sat down beside her. "I don't want us to be angry with each other. I want you to have a nice birthday."

"Then let me invite Donny."

"Maybe some other time . . . when you're

older. There must be someone else you'd enjoy taking to the theater."

Emily rolled over and thought about it. "Molly."

"Who's she?"

"Don't you remember? My best friend at camp."

"But you haven't seen her since last summer. Do you know where she lives?"

"We took the train together and we were in the same cabin."

Her mother sighed deeply. "All right. I'll call the director and see what I can do."

A few days later when Emily came home from school, her mother gave her a piece of paper with a number on it and said it was Molly's. Excitedly Emily ran to the telephone in her parents' bedroom and called.

"Hello," someone said on the other end of the line.

"I want to talk to Molly."

"This is Molly."

Her voice sounded different on the phone. Emily felt shy. "It's me, Emily."

Molly let out a whoop and they both started chattering at once as though they were back in their cabin at camp. Finally Emily remembered why she had called and invited her to the show.

"Hold on," Molly said, "while I ask my mother."

Emily waited in suspense. She sat on the very edge of the bed, twisting and untwisting the telephone cord. She hadn't realized how much she had missed Molly until she heard her voice.

When she came back on the line and shouted, "I can come!" Emily knew it was going to be her best birthday ever.

Emily woke up on May twelfth with the feeling that wonderful things were going to happen. She was fourteen.

In the kitchen her mother was making fruit salad. "Happy birthday, darling." She kissed Emily.

The coffee cooking on the stove smelled good. "Where's Daddy?" Emily asked.

"At the store. He'll be back soon."

Emily drank her juice. "What's the fruit salad for?"

"Your birthday dinner party. Tom and

Phyllis and Jessica are coming over when we get back from the show. We're going to a matinee." Emily's mother opened the refrigerator and took out a carton of milk.

"I don't want milk," Emily said firmly. "I want coffee."

"What?" Her mother looked surprised.

Emily was surprised too but the words kept coming out of her mouth. "I hate milk. I want to drink coffee like you and Tom and Phyllis and Daddy."

"You're too young."

"I am not. I'm almost in high school. Tom started drinking coffee when he was my age."

"You're not Tom."

"Donny drinks coffee."

"I don't care what other children do."

Emily stood up and put her arms around her mother's waist. "Please? It'll be my best birthday present."

Her mother hugged her and poured her a cup. Emily added milk and two spoonfuls of sugar. The coffee didn't taste as good as it smelled but it felt grown-up to be sipping it.

After breakfast she got dressed in her party

clothes—a new flowered dress with a lace collar, and the shoes she had bought with Phyllis. She studied herself in the mirror. Did she look any older? No. Maybe it was her hair. She had always worn it the same way—shoulder length with bangs. Suddenly she hated it and wanted short hair like Phyllis's.

From the hallway her father called, "Where's the baby?"

Emily knew he meant her and ran out to hug him. He carried the mail and an armful of bags from the delicatessen. She could smell the pickles.

"Something came for you." He gave her an envelope.

The handwriting looked familiar. Emily unsealed the flap and pulled out a birthday card with a funny picture of an elephant making a cake. The message said, "To Emily from Donny." Emily's cheeks grew warm. She hugged the card to her, then read it again.

"Who's it from?" her mother asked.

"Donny."

His name hung in the air between them.

"Who's Donny?" her father said.

"One of Emily's friends at school. Come on, Irv. Let's get dressed or we'll be late for the show."

Before they left they gave Emily her present. She knew from the size and shape of the little box it was jewelry. Her heart thumped. Could it be earrings for pierced ears, like Phyllis's?

Breathlessly she took off the lid. Inside, nestled on a piece of cotton, was something gold. It was an initial necklace with the letter E. Emily was so disappointed she thought she'd cry.

Her father must have known because his face fell. "Don't you like it, sugar? I can take it back and get something else."

"I wanted earrings for pierced ears."

"You're not old enough."

"I am! I'm fourteen!"

"Next you'll be wanting to drive, I suppose."

"Maybe," Emily said.

"Let's see how the necklace looks on." Emily's mother fastened the clasp. Then she took Emily's face in her hands and said tenderly, "You're our gift of gold."

"I don't want to be that anymore," Emily shouted. "I want to be grown-up!"

"Listen, young lady," her father began.

"Irv, let's go," her mother interrupted, "or we'll be late for the theater."

When they drove up to Molly's building she was standing outside waiting for them. At first Emily couldn't believe her eyes. Molly had the same red hair and smiling face but she looked much older, more like Cheryl and Amanda. Her braids were gone. Now her hair was long with some curls and she had grown out her bangs. She was wearing a strapless dress with an elasticized tube top and a skirt that fluffed out at the bottom. On her feet were pumps with little heels that matched her party purse. Compared to her, Emily felt like a baby in her buttoned-up flowery dress.

Her mother must have noticed Molly's dress too because she said, "Won't you be cold in the theater, dear? I think it's air-conditioned."

"I never get cold." Molly climbed into the back seat of the car. "I'm always hot."

Emily's mother gave her father a look, but neither of them said anything.

From her purse Molly took a small package. "Happy birthday, Emily."

"What is it?"

"Open it."

Emily pulled off the ribbon and tore off the paper. Inside was a dark blue bottle of perfume.

"Thanks!" She hugged Molly. "I'll put some on right now." When she opened the bottle there was a strong smell like lots of flowers in the florist's shop. Her father rolled his window all the way down.

Molly touched Emily's necklace. "Is that new? I like it."

"I like your fingernails." They were painted a shade of pink that matched Molly's lip gloss.

"My sister let me borrow her polish," Molly said.

"Is that her dress?"

Molly laughed. "No, it's mine." She settled back and said, "What boys in your class are cute?"

In a lowered voice Emily told her about Donny. Talking about him was almost as good as being with him. "I wanted to invite him today," she said, "but my mother wouldn't let me. Now I'm glad you came, Molly."

"Is he your boyfriend?"

Emily flushed. "I don't know."

"I have a boyfriend," Molly said, and told her about him while they rode downtown.

At the theater there was a big crowd of people. Emily held Molly's hand so they wouldn't get lost. Her father bought a program and an usher showed them to their seats, close to the stage.

Over the sound of the orchestra tuning up Molly said, "Look at that boy over there."

"Where?" Emily asked.

Molly grabbed her arm and pointed to the front row. "Over there, dummy. Sitting down next to the lady in the green dress."

Emily looked where she was pointing and saw a teenage boy with lots of curly hair. He didn't look as nice as Donny. But Molly thought she knew him. She jumped up and ran down the aisle and Emily followed her.

"Get back here," Emily's father called but she ignored him. Then she felt his hand on her shoulder. He grabbed Molly too and steered them back to their seats. "I want you both to sit down," he said sternly, "and behave yourselves."

The man sitting in front of them turned around and stared at Emily. She smiled at him.

Her father said something to her mother.

"Relax, Irv," she said. "It doesn't mean anything."

All at once the house lights dimmed and the music began. Emily shivered with excitement and squeezed Molly's hand. When the curtain went up she said, "There's the girl from the program. It's Annie!" Annie seemed to be their age but she was dressed in rags. Emily felt sorry for her.

"Where's her red dress and perm?" Molly said.

"Shh." The man in front of them turned around and glowered.

Emily's mother leaned over. "Girls, save your talking for later."

Onstage some other girls in raggy clothes sang and danced, then Annie sang a song about wanting a mommy and daddy.

Emily nudged Molly with her elbow. "I know that song."

"Will you girls be quiet," the man in front of them snarled, "or do I have to call the usher?

People shouldn't bring unsuitable children to the theater!"

"Mind your own business," Emily's father said.

People around them hissed, *"Shhh!"*

Emily's mother leaned over again and muttered between clenched teeth, "Girls, you really must be quiet till intermission!"

At the end of the act, when the lights came on, Emily's mother led the way to the ladies' room. She sat on a bench and read the program while Emily and Molly stood in line.

"I have the curse," Molly whispered.

"What's that?" Emily asked.

"You know, my period."

Their turn came and they went into two adjoining stalls. When they came out and went to the sinks Emily said, "You can have babies too. My sister-in-law said taking off your top is part of it. You were right."

"Who wants babies?" Molly rinsed her hands. "I want boyfriends. When I grow up I want to do it for fun."

"Fun!" Emily thought about what Phyllis and her mother had told her. "What's fun about that?" she said.

Molly snatched a paper towel from the dispenser. "Are you retarded or something?" she said jokingly.

Emily stiffened. "Don't call me that."

"You know," Molly said. "Fun is when you kiss naked and everything."

"What do you mean 'everything'?"

Women standing in line waiting for the stalls turned their heads and stared at Molly and Emily. One woman said something to the girl behind her and they both laughed.

"Haven't you ever heard of getting to third base?" Molly said.

"Do you mean baseball?"

"No, silly. Your parents did it to have you!"

"They never did anything," Emily declared indignantly.

"Yes, they did," Molly said with authority, "and so did your brother and sister-in-law."

Emily wadded her paper towel and threw it away. "How do you know? Phyllis and Tom love each other and are married. They got very close at the right time."

"You don't have to be married. People do that for fun. My sister told me." Molly flounced off to the mirrors framed with many bulbs.

Emily trotted alongside her. "I don't believe it. Phyllis never said anything about fun." Fun was laughing and dancing and playing dress-up.

"Ask anyone," Molly said. "Ask your sister-in-law. It's true." She fished through her purse for her lip gloss and put some on.

Emily watched. She wanted lip gloss too.

"I have this magazine I found in my sister's wastebasket." Molly dropped her voice to a whisper. "It has pictures of naked men."

A gray-haired woman powdering her nose at the next mirror glanced at them.

Emily gasped in horror.

"I'll show it to you when you come over sometime."

"Molly," Emily said in a whisper, "a boy did something bad to me."

"What boy?" Molly sounded excited.

"Patrick. You don't know him. He lives on my block."

"What did he do?"

"He . . . touched me and kissed me." Remembering it made Emily feel sick.

"What's so bad about that? He likes you."

"Likes me!"

Molly fluffed her hair and admired herself in the mirror. "Emily, boys do that when they like a girl."

"Donny doesn't. He sent me a birthday card."

"Don't you want to have boyfriends?" Molly said. "Boys won't like you if you don't fool around."

"Can't you do something else if you like a boy?"

"Like what? Gee, Emily, sometimes you act like a big baby."

Emily stood there thinking about it. "No, Molly. You're wrong. Donny likes me. He doesn't want to fool around. He's my friend."

Molly groaned.

Then Emily asked, "Can I borrow your lip gloss?"

"Sure."

It smelled and tasted like strawberries. Emily rubbed her lips together the way she had seen her mother and Phyllis do. "How do I look?"

"Great."

A gong sounded and Emily's mother walked

toward them saying, "Time to go back to—"
She broke off when she saw Emily. "What do
you have on your mouth?"

"Lip gloss."

"Where did you get it?"

"Molly." Emily's cheeks burned.

"You'd better wipe some off before your
father sees you." Emily's mother handed her
a tissue.

When they got back to their row Emily's
father said, "What took you so long?"

"Tell you later," Emily's mother said, slip-
ping past him.

During the rest of the show Emily's mind
wandered. She kept thinking about what
Molly had told her. Every time she tried to
picture Tom and Phyllis kissing naked, her
mind went blank.

On the way home Molly talked more about
her boyfriend. Emily wanted to ask her what
getting to third base meant but she noticed her
parents were listening. When they dropped
Molly off she thanked them for a nice time and
said, "Can Emily sleep over at my house next
Saturday?"

"Can I?"

"We'll see," Emily's mother said in the tone of voice that meant she probably couldn't.

Later, at home, Emily's parents went into their bedroom to change out of their good clothes. From her room Emily could hear them talking.

"Wasn't she a little wild and boy crazy?" her father said.

Her mother shushed him but Emily knew they were talking about Molly. Then they started talking about her. She overheard the same old phrases—"growing up," "who will take care of her?"

Didn't they *want* her to be fourteen? She did. She wanted to have pierced ears and wear lip gloss and nail polish. She wanted to be grown-up like other girls. Why couldn't she be? What was wrong with her?

She looked at herself in the mirror and tried to see. She knew there was something not right about her. But what was it? She moved closer to the mirror and looked very hard into her own eyes but she couldn't see what it was. She started to cry and the doorbell rang.

12

〰〰〰

From the hallway Phyllis called, "Where's the birthday girl?"

Emily ran into her arms and hugged her tight. "I've got to talk to you. My friend Molly told me about—"

Phyllis sniffed. "What smells?"

"Molly gave me perfume for my birthday."

"Come see what we got for you."

In the living room packages wrapped in light blue paper and tied with yellow yarn filled the coffee table.

"Happy birthday, honey." Tom was holding Jessica. "Open your presents."

"All for me?" Emily opened them and thrilled at the surprises—Chinese slippers, a red cloth flower that pinned on, and a shoulder bag like the kind Cheryl and Amanda wore.

She thanked Tom and Phyllis with big hugs, and they all sat down at the table. Emily's mother passed platters of cheese and meat while her father poured bubbly wine for the grown-ups.

"How about a taste for Emily?" Tom said as her father held the bottle poised over the glasses. "It's her birthday."

Emily's mother gave him a look. "All right, but just a thimbleful."

Emily's father gave her some and raised his glass. "To our precious baby."

"Don't call me that!"

"Emily . . ." Her mother threw her a look.

Emily clinked glasses with everyone and took a sip. The bubbles stung her nose.

"Boy, I'm starving." Phyllis attacked the potato salad.

Emily leaned over and said in a hushed voice, "Phyllis, I've got to talk to you. It's real important."

"What?"

Emily cupped her hand around Phyllis's ear and whispered, "Something Molly said about getting to third base and fooling around."

"Emily," her mother said, "it's rude to tell secrets in front of other people."

"Later, honey," Phyllis said. "Let's eat before Jessica gets fussy." She helped herself to turkey and rye bread. "Tell me about the show. Did you like it?"

"Donny sent me a birthday card."

"He did? I want to see it after dinner."

When they were done eating, Emily's mother went into the kitchen and came back carrying a birthday cake with all the candles burning. Tom turned off the lights and everyone sang "Happy Birthday."

"Make a wish," Phyllis said.

Emily wondered if she dared wish for what she really wanted. Would it come true?

"Hurry up," Tom said. "The candles are melting the icing."

Quickly Emily wished for pierced ears and earrings so that she'd look like a regular teenage girl when she went to high school. And last of all, she wished for what she always wished for—a baby of her own. Then she took a deep breath and blew as hard as she could.

"Hurrah!" Phyllis clapped her hands.

Tom cut the cake and served Emily first. Just as she was taking a bite the doorbell rang.

"Who could that be?" her father said.

The doorbell rang again.

"Irv, see who it is." Emily's mother started to pour coffee.

Emily followed her father into the hall. When he opened the door her knees started shaking and her heart raced.

"Hi," Donny said. "I've come to see Emily." He stood in the doorway holding a bag of potato chips.

Emily had never seen him so dressed up. He wore a button-up denim shirt, khakis, and black Doc Martens boots. His hair looked wet. Emily guessed he must have jelled it.

She stepped forward to greet him.

"Happy birthday, Emily."

"Thanks. I got your card today. How did you know it was my birthday?"

Emily's father was speechless. When her mother rushed into the hallway he turned to her. "Did you invite him here?"

She took him aside and lowered her voice. "Be gracious. He probably came to give Emily a present." In her regular voice she said, "Please come in."

He wiped his feet on the doormat and walked into the apartment. Emily couldn't believe he was there.

Her father looked him over. "He probably doesn't have time to stay. His parents must want him to come right back."

"No, I can stay." Donny gave the bag of chips to Emily's mother.

"Thank you," she said. "Emily, introduce us to your friend."

Emily's elbow itched and her stomach felt funny. "This is Donny."

"So, this is Donny." Emily's mother smiled at him. "You're just in time for birthday cake."

"How did you get here?" Emily asked.

"On the bus."

"You ride the bus by yourself?" Emily's father seemed surprised. "How long have you been doing that?"

"Since I was twelve."

"That's very nice." Emily's mother patted her hair.

"How did you know where I lived?" Emily said.

Donny grinned. "I looked at your address card and remembered the numbers. My aunt told me to take the number four bus. Sometimes I take it when I play basketball in the park."

Emily thought Donny was really great.

"Let's go back to the party." Emily's mother led the way to the dining alcove.

At the table Phyllis winked at Emily. "Who's your friend?"

"This is Donny."

Tom shook hands with him and introduced Phyllis and Jessica.

"Cute baby," Donny said.

From her car seat Jessica stared up at him with her big brown eyes and blew bubbles.

Emily's mother said, "Irv, get Donny a chair. Emily, get another plate and fork."

Emily's father clomped to the hall closet and brought back a folding bridge chair while Emily set a place for Donny next to her. Her father shot Donny a suspicious glance as he opened the chair. Donny seemed almost afraid to sit down.

Why was her father being so unfriendly? At school they were always nice when they gave chairs to visitors.

Her mother served Donny a piece of cake. He took a bite. "This is good. I like chocolate."

"I'm so glad." Emily's mother went into the kitchen.

Her father said nothing and ate his cake in silence. Emily's mother brought back two glasses of milk.

"Can't Donny and I have coffee?" Emily asked.

Her father scowled. "Since when have these kids been drinking coffee?"

"Since this morning. Mommy said it was OK."

"Isabelle, do you think that's a good idea? Isn't she a little young?"

"Irv, we'll talk about it later." Emily's mother came back with mugs. Her hands shook as she poured coffee for Donny and Emily.

"I like lots of milk and sugar in mine." Donny reached for the creamer.

"Me too," Emily chirped.

"She's fourteen and suddenly she's grown-up?" Emily's father said to Emily's mother.

"Irv," she said in that tone of voice, "stop it. I don't want to talk about it right now. Just let it be."

At the sound of their angry voices Jessica started to cry.

"She can't be hungry." Phyllis turned to Tom. "I fed her before we came."

"There, there." Tom put a pacifier in the baby's mouth but she spit it out and howled. He unfastened her strap and picked her up, holding her close, but she kept crying.

"We'd better go." Phyllis leapt up so fast she knocked over her mug.

"It's OK, it's OK." Emily's mother mopped up coffee with napkins.

"Ready when you are." Tom put the screaming Jessica back in her car seat and buckled her in while Phyllis gathered up the blanket and diaper bag.

"Can't you stay?" Emily's mother pleaded. "I'll walk the baby."

"Please don't go," Emily begged.

"We really have to," Phyllis said. "Jessica's been cranky all day. She'll do better at home in her own crib. Emily, I'll see you another time."

"Nice to have met you." Tom shook Donny's hand again.

"I'll help you with all that stuff." Emily's father got up and left too.

Now Donny and Emily were the only ones

at the table. Her eyes swept over the wreck-
age—plates of half-eaten cake, mugs of cold
coffee, soggy crumpled napkins. Tears came
to her eyes and she couldn't swallow the piece
of cake in her mouth. This was the worst birthday she had ever had. Everything was going
wrong. She bet Donny wished he had never
come.

"Emily," her mother said with a quavering
voice. She began to clear. "Why don't you
bring your postcards into the living room and
show them to Donny."

Emily pulled Donny's arm, glad to get him
out of there. She carried her heavy carton of
postcards from the bedroom into the living
room and dropped it on the floor with a thud.
"Want to see Asbury Park?"

"Maybe later." Donny took something out
of his pocket. "This is for you."

It was two barrettes with little red hearts
attached to a card.

"They're so pretty. Thanks, Donny. This
is my best present."

"I bought them with my own money."

"I'll save them so they won't break."

"No. Wear them."

With trembling fingers Emily unclasped the barrettes and fastened them in her hair.

Donny gazed at her, beaming. "They look nice."

He took her hand and held it. For a moment everything was OK again. As they stood there holding hands Emily felt warm and safe and happy.

From the hall she heard her parents saying good-night to Phyllis and Tom. When the front door closed they started whispering. Their voices got lower and lower, the way they always did when they argued about her. Emily strained to hear what they were saying but couldn't. She let go of Donny's hand.

Her father stomped into the living room, sank into his big green chair, and started reading the newspaper.

Donny glanced sideways at him. "Mr. Gold, this sure is a nice apartment."

Emily's father didn't answer. The only sound was the turning of pages.

"Emily has lots of good postcards." He held up one showing the Statue of Liberty.

"Don't you have to go home now, young man?" Emily's father said to Donny.

"No, sir." Donny checked his watch. "Not yet."

"Well, I think it's time."

Emily froze. She watched in horror as her father jumped up, took Donny by the arm and walked him to the front door.

"Daddy!" Emily ran after them.

Donny gave her a helpless look over his shoulder. "See you at school."

When the front door slammed Emily was choked with rage. She grabbed her father's sleeve. "Why did you do that?" she shouted in his face.

Her father took a step back.

She repeated, "Why did you do that?"

Her father walked toward the living room. Emily followed.

"You're too young to have boyfriends," he grumbled.

"He's *not* my boyfriend," Emily shrieked. "He's my friend!"

Her father turned and bent toward her. His body looked tight and angry. "Calm down," he said. "Emily, you don't understand. You can't trust boys."

She clenched her fists. "I can trust Donny,"

she shouted. "He's nice to me. You just don't want me to have any friends."

"That's not true. And you stop shouting at me, young lady." He shook his finger in her face. "Boys are after only one thing."

"What?" She planted her feet apart and put her hands on her hips.

Her father angrily waved his hand. "You just don't understand."

"You let Tom bring friends to the house!" Emily screamed. "Boys *and* girls."

"That was different."

"Why?" She quavered. She knew the answer already and hated her father for it.

"Emily, simmer down." He dropped into his green chair and picked up the paper.

She grabbed the paper. He held on to it. It ripped.

"I know why!" she yelled. "It's because my head doesn't work right. That's it, isn't it?" Tears streamed down her face.

"Now, honey. Now, honey. Isabelle!" he shouted. "Come in here." He reached out and took Emily's arm.

She twisted away and jabbed at him with her elbow.

"Isabelle!" he called again.

But before her mother came in, Emily ran to her room, sobbing. She flung herself onto the bed.

Then an idea came to her.

Maybe she'd run away from home.

13

AFTER SCHOOL ON MONDAY EMILY SAID TO HER
mother, "I want to go down and get the mail."

"By yourself?" Her mother looked up from
the checks she was writing at the table in the
dining alcove.

Emily knew it was the only way she could
go out alone. "Mommy! I'm fourteen!"

"Lower your voice. I know perfectly well
how old you are, but you've never gone by
yourself before."

"You never let me do anything. You and
Daddy treat me like a baby." She still hadn't
forgiven him for ruining her birthday. They
hadn't talked since that night. She wouldn't
even give him a good-night kiss anymore.

"Are you expecting a letter?"

"I don't know." Emily scratched a mosquito
bite on her arm. "Maybe."

Her mother hesitated. "If I let you go will you come right back?"

"Yes," Emily lied.

Her mother reached into her purse on the floor beside her for the keys and singled out a small slim one. "This is for the mailbox. Now don't lose it, and be sure to lock the box after you take out the mail."

"OK."

"And when you get the mail bring it to me. Don't wander off. Do you understand?"

Emily nodded and took the bunch of keys. On the way to the front door she stopped in her room for her new purse and slung it over her shoulder. Maybe she'd see Cheryl and Amanda in the lobby. They could tell her which bus to take downtown and which one to take back in case she changed her mind. She emptied her bank on her bed and scooped up all the money. It must be a lot, she thought, because when she dumped the coins into her purse, her purse felt heavy and clanked with every step she took.

She bounded out the front door and closed it shut behind her. Silently she said good-bye to her apartment and rode the elevator downstairs. Feeling grown-up and pleased with herself, she strolled past the mailboxes and outside into the May sunshine to look for Cheryl and Amanda. Overhead a breeze stirred the leaves on a skinny tree planted in front of her building. The light green leaves just beginning to unfold were wonderful.

The beep of a car horn made her jump. Shading her eyes with her hand she looked around and saw the red car that often drove past her building. She recognized the rainbow sticker in the back window and the painting of flames on the hood. The car pulled up to the curb and rolled to a stop.

There were two teenage boys inside. The one behind the steering wheel had tight curly hair and a little moustache. He leaned out and waved to her. Emily waved back. Then he motioned for her to come over.

Her parents and teachers always said, "Never talk to strangers," but this boy wasn't really a stranger because she had seen him before.

She skipped over to the open car window and her purse made a tinkling sound.

"Do you know where Cheryl is?" the boy asked.

"Nope."

"Have you seen her?"

"I just came out," Emily said.

He whispered something to the other boy who was wearing big baggy shorts and a baseball cap backwards. Then he rested his arm on the door. Over the low hum of the engine idling he said, "How about coming for a ride?"

Emily scratched her mosquito bite. "I don't know."

"What's your name?"

"Emily."

"How old are you?"

"Fourteen," she said proudly.

The boy smiled. "You're cuter than Cheryl."

"Thanks." Emily felt herself blush.

"This is a nice car," the boy with the moustache said. He switched on the radio to some rock music and made it real loud. "You like that?"

Emily did, but she remembered her parents' and teachers' warnings. "I'm not supposed to go in anybody's car."

"We're not anybody," the boy said. "I'm Artie and he's Chick. We're friends of Cheryl and Amanda."

"You are?" Emily's eyes widened.

"Yeah. We go to the same high school."

Emily wished she went there too.

Artie opened the door a little. "Take a look."

Emily peeked. The inside of the car was also red. Big black-and-white dice hung from the mirror. Leopard skin covered the seats. She had never seen a car like that before.

"Sit in it for a minute," Artie said.

Emily stood there trying to make up her mind. Maybe Chick and Artie could give her a ride downtown. Then she wouldn't have to worry about taking a bus and figuring out where to get on, and where to get off, and how much money to pay.

"We won't hurt you," Artie said. "Don't you trust us?"

Trust. Phyllis had used that word. "There are nice boys and not-so-nice boys," she had said. "You have to know which boys you can trust."

Emily wondered if she should trust Artie and Chick. Were they nice? They seemed friendly. She looked around. There was no one on the street. It reminded her of that time with Patrick.

"Aw, what's the matter, Emily? Don't you like me?" Artie talked in a funny voice. "Don't you think I'm cute, just a little teeny bit?"

Emily giggled. Artie was nicer than Patrick.

"Come on," he coaxed. "It'll be fun."

Fun. Molly had said people "did it" for fun and she would when she grew up. Her voice had sounded just like Artie's when she had said it. She had had the same look on her face. A smile that wasn't really a smile. A smile that meant trouble.

"My mommy's waiting for me."

Artie checked his watch. "We'll take you around the block and come right back."

Come right back. Emily's mother had said that. She was probably waiting for Emily now. How sad she would be when Emily never came back. Her father too. But it was his fault she was going away.

"OK." Emily started toward the door on the passenger side.

Chick moved over to make room for her.

With her fingers on the handle of the door, Emily glanced at Artie. The grin on his face gave her a funny feeling in her stomach and she froze.

Patrick had grinned at her like that the time she wore the red sweater. Donny never looks at me like that, she thought.

All of a sudden she turned and made a dash for her building.

"Hey, come back!" Artie called.

But Emily didn't stop running until she reached the mailboxes. Her fingers shook as she fitted the key into the lock of the box marked "Irving and Isabelle Gold." Quickly she pulled out bills, letters, and a catalogue, locked the box, and raced up the four flights of stairs. She burst into the apartment. Her mother came tearing out of the bedroom. Her face was white.

"Emily, where have you been? I was on the phone with Phyllis. I was just going to come down and look for you."

Emily ran into her mother's arms and wanted to stay there forever, but her mother drew back and started asking questions.

"Where did you go? What happened?"

"Some boys wanted to take me for a ride."

"What boys?" Her mother's eyes narrowed. "What are their names?"

"Chick and Artie."

"Oh, my goodness." Her mother collapsed

into a chair in the dining alcove and rubbed her forehead as though she had a headache. "Why were you talking to strangers?"

"They're not strangers. I've seen them before. They're friends of Cheryl's. But they're not *my* friends. I didn't trust them."

"Oh, Emily. You told me you'd get the mail and come right back."

"Here it is." Emily held out her handful of bills and letters.

Her mother got up and hugged her tight, kissing her hair. "What a smart girl you are! You used such good judgment. Wait till Daddy hears. He'll be so proud of you."

Emily wasn't sure.

When her father came home for dinner her mother told him what had happened as soon as he walked into the hallway.

"You see?" he exploded. "This just proves she's not ready for boys. What's Chick's last name? What's Artie's last name? I'm going to call their parents." He put down his big brown jeweler's bag and headed for the phone in the kitchen. "I told you you were too young, Emily. All this talk about being grown-up is a bunch of . . . nonsense!"

Emily blocked his way and faced him. "I

am too ready," she said quietly. "The boys didn't hurt me. I knew what to do. I used good judgment. Mommy said so."

"That's right," her mother added. "Our girl handled herself just beautifully. She really did, Irv."

"I knew I couldn't trust them and I came straight home." Emily left out the part about running away. Maybe she'd tell them another time. Maybe never.

Her father grew quiet also. He stood there in the dining alcove and looked her straight in the eye for what seemed like a long time. Then the corners of his mouth turned up in a small smile. A smile that said he was wrong and she was right. He put his arm around Emily. "You've got a good head on your shoulders, kiddo."

It was the best thing he had ever said to her. She brushed his cheek with a kiss. It was the first kiss she had given him since her birthday and she meant it.

After dinner she called Molly and told her about Chick and Artie.

"Emily, you should have gone in their car," Molly said. "It would have been fun."

"I don't think so," Emily said. Fun was drawing and dancing with Donny. Fun was holding Jessica and taking her for a walk in the park. Fun was feeling safe.

"*I* would have gone," Molly said. "If you see them again, tell them my name."

"No, I won't," Emily said. Maybe Molly didn't know everything after all.

When she went to Phyllis's the next day she told her all about Chick and Artie.

"Good for you," Phyllis said. "You were so smart not to trust them."

"They weren't my friends," Emily said. "I think they wanted to fool around."

"Terrific! That's exactly what I meant." Phyllis beamed. "I *knew* you'd get it."

She was standing at the table folding Jessica's baby clothes and stacking them in piles. "Emily, do you think you could listen for Jessica while I hop into the shower? It will only take a minute."

"Sure," Emily said.

"I think she's asleep." Phyllis carried the baby clothes into the bedroom and put them on the bottom shelf of the changing table.

Emily followed her on tiptoe and peeked

into the crib. Sure enough, Jessica was curled up in a corner, her head pressed against the polka-dot bumper. Her eyes were tightly shut.

"If she cries," Phyllis said softly, "come get me." She grabbed some clean underwear, shorts, and a T-shirt and headed for the bathroom.

Emily sat on the edge of the bed listening. She was thrilled to finally be taking care of the baby by herself. From the bathroom came the sound of running water. Above the noise of the shower Emily heard a little cough. She went to the crib and leaned over the rail. Jessica squirmed and yawned. Her eyes were still shut, though. Emily stood there watching her. Someday she'd have a baby of her own, just like Jessica.

All of a sudden Jessica let out a cry. Then another. The noise startled Emily and made her jump. Jessica moved her head side to side and cried louder. Emily patted her back. "There, there," she cooed.

But the baby didn't stop crying. She cried louder. How could such a small creature make so much noise? Emily's heart pounded in terror. Maybe she had done something wrong.

She ran to the bathroom and knocked on the door. "Phyllis! Jessica's up."

Emily raced back into the bedroom and over to the crib. Now Jessica was screaming. Her face was all red. Her body trembled. She spread her tiny fingers. From the floor came the sound of thumping. Mrs. Shoeman and her broom. Emily stamped her foot. "Stop it! Stop it, you old witch." But the thumping didn't stop. Neither did the crying.

Emily wrapped Jessica's receiving blanket around her and awkwardly picked her up. The blanket was bunched up and Jessica's legs stuck out of it. There was a bad smell. Green stuff oozed out of Jessica's diaper and trickled down her leg. Some of it smeared on Emily's arm. The baby stiffened. Emily was afraid she'd drop her. Where could she put the baby? Back in the crib? On the bed? She didn't know what to do. Her heart beat fast. Her mouth went dry. She didn't want to be holding this baby anymore.

"Phyllis! Phyllis!" she yelled.

Phyllis came running into the room. A towel was wrapped around her and knotted in front. Drops of water still clung to her shoulders.

"What happened? I told you not to pick her up!" she said angrily. She took the screaming baby and cradled her in her arms.

Emily started to cry. It was like the time she had watered her wedding present plant right after Jessica was born. Only this was worse.

"I'm sorry, Em," Phyllis said in a kinder voice. "I didn't mean that the way it sounded."

But Emily knew she did and she knew why. "Oh, Phyllis, I thought I could take care of her. But she got all stiff. And she was yelling—"

Phyllis stood close to her. "It's OK. You came to get me. That was the right thing to do. Sometimes I make mistakes too. This morning I burned the oatmeal."

"But that's just cereal. This was Jessica. I couldn't do it. I'll never be able to take care of a baby all by myself." Emily hid her face in her hands and wept.

14

⁄⁄⁄⁄⁄⁄⁄⁄

BEFORE GRADUATION A LETTER ARRIVED FROM Emily's new high school. She worried. Maybe they weren't going to admit her after all. Maybe she wasn't smart enough or grown-up enough. What if she didn't graduate and stayed at her old school forever?

That night at dinner her mother read the letter aloud to Emily and her father.

This is to inform you that your daughter, Emily Gold, has been approved to participate in the sheltered workshop situation. We are planning to have her receive vocational training at the Goodwill Industries Workshop. Enclosed please find . . .

Emily stopped listening. Her feet got cold and she lost her appetite. *Sheltered.* She knew that word. This was it. They were going to send her away. All of those whispered conversations she had overheard meant only one thing—she was too much trouble. They didn't want her anymore.

Emily's mother folded the letter. "Did you understand it?"

Tears came to Emily's eyes. Surely this was one of her last dinners at home. Never again would she eat tuna fish salad and blintzes on a warm night in June. She looked down at her lap and tried not to cry. "You're sending me away."

"No, *no*, darling. Whatever gave you that idea?"

"The letter said so. You're sending me where Theo went."

"Who's this Theo?" her father said. "She's always talking about Theo."

"He was in Mrs. Polarski's class for a long time." Emily twisted her napkin. "Then he got sent to a home for kids who are too much trouble."

"This is your home," her father said. "You'll stay here as long as I have a breath in my body!"

"We love you." Her mother leaned over and stroked her hair. "You're our Emily, good as gold. The letter has exciting news. You're going to learn how to do a job, just like Daddy and Tom. You'll go to a new place to work with other students from your high school and then you'll come home on the bus the way you always have."

Emily snuffled and brushed away a tear. "What kind of job?"

Her mother scanned the second page of the letter. "You can choose it yourself . . . working in the cafeteria—you're good at that—packaging silverware for airplanes, sorting jewelry—"

"Jewelry!" Emily lit up. "I'd like that." For a long time she had wanted to work in her daddy's shop.

"Good. We'll tell them when we sign the consent slip. You'll start in a couple of weeks at summer school."

"Summer school. But what about camp and Molly?"

"Darling, this is more important. It's a good way for you to get used to your new school and job."

The night before graduation Molly called

Emily and asked her what she was going to wear. She told Molly about the letter.

"I'm going to the Goodwill Workshop too!" Molly squealed.

"Are you going to do jewelry?" Emily asked.

"I haven't decided yet."

"Molly, I've decided something."

"What?"

In a lowered voice Emily said, "I'm not going to have a baby." She swallowed hard. "Not for a long, long time."

"That's good. When did you change your mind?"

"It's not because of the gross thing." Emily told her about taking care of Jessica while Phyllis was in the shower. "The baby screamed. I didn't know what to do. I don't think I can do it by myself. But maybe someday . . ."

And suddenly she thought, My baby will also have a daddy. We could take care of it together. Maybe someday . . .

On the morning of graduation Emily's parents got dressed up and drove her to school. In the car she tried not to think about saying good-bye to Donny.

He was already in the classroom when she

arrived. Mr. Davis helped them count their stars and let them pick prizes. Emily got the perfume-bottle necklace and put it on right away. Donny chose the baseball cap and put it on too.

Today he looked different. He wore a long-sleeved white shirt and a red tie that matched his cap. Emily had never seen him wear a tie before. He looked very grown-up.

"Donny, you look nice."

"So do you. I'm glad you're wearing the barrettes I gave you."

She grinned at his approval.

When it was time to go to the auditorium Emily filed in with the girls and Donny marched in with the boys. She searched the audience for her family and spotted all of them. Jessica was sitting in Phyllis's lap. Emily was almost embarrassed when her father stood up and waved. She waved back, just a little, barely lifting her hand.

After the speeches and songs Emily's class went up on stage, one by one, to receive their diplomas. When it was Emily's turn her father cheered loudly and her family kept clapping as the next name was called.

Later, out in the hall, she found them. Phyllis gave her a big hug and admired her perfume bottle necklace. "Jessica wants to congratulate you too." She put the drooling baby into Emily's arms.

Emily held Jessica and blew kisses to her. The baby started to laugh and coo. Emily hugged her and blew kisses again.

"Look, she's smiling," Phyllis said. "Emily, she loves you. She loves her aunt."

Emily gave Jessica a kiss, then returned her to Phyllis before her flowery dress got messed up.

From his jacket pocket her father took out a small box and handed it to her. Inside was a pair of star-shaped earrings for pierced ears. They were exactly like Phyllis's.

Emily couldn't believe her eyes. "Can I have my ears pierced?"

Her mother nodded. "We'll call and make an appointment as soon as we get home."

"Emily," her father said in a teary voice, "you're really growing up." He gave her a hug but it was a new kind. Gentle and quick.

"Thank you!" Emily kissed her parents, then looked for Donny. There he was, standing and talking with someone. She rushed over to congratulate him and he introduced her to his aunt.

"Emily, it's a pleasure to meet you."

Emily choked up. Maybe this was the last time she'd see Donny for a long time, maybe never. They stood close to each other, almost touching.

"I'm going to miss you, Donny."

"I can come over and see you."

"What about my father?"

"He's OK."

"Donny, I won't be home."

He looked panicked. "Where are you going?"

"Summer school and the sheltered workshop."

"Me too!"

"You are?"

"I'm going to work in a real cafeteria downtown."

Their eyes met and she thought she'd burst with happiness.

While they bubbled with plans Emily's father came over.

Uh-oh, Emily thought. Now he's going to

spoil everything. Her heart pounded and she tightened her grip on her earring box.

But to her surprise her father introduced himself to Donny's aunt and gave her a friendly smile. "Would you and Donny like to join us for lunch?"

Emily relaxed.

Donny turned to her. "Do you want me to?"

"Of course I do. You're one of my best friends." She took his arm and led the way. I have a friend named Donny, she said to herself. I'm fourteen. I'm going to high school and I'll work in the jewelry department.

I'm Emily good as gold.